"I give up. I'm wav— announced. *"I'm al—*

Joy's heart did a funny little flip-flop at Declan's choice of words. But she was determined to ignore it. She could not, however, stop her smile. "You've decided to let me help you make some changes in your life, follow my antistress program?"

"I'm not happy about it, but yes—"

"Oh, Declan, I'm so glad."

He felt his body tighten as he watched her smile fade. "Why?" he asked in a raspy voice.

"Because I . . ." Because she didn't want anything to happen to him. Because she couldn't think straight when he looked at her like that. Because . . . oh, darn it, just because.

He lifted a hand and drew his thumb across her lips. "You have the most kissable mouth I have ever seen." He moved closer, lowering his head toward hers. "I'm going to go mad if I don't kiss you, Joy."

Her mind shouted no, but her heart raced with pleasure. He cradled her face in his hands and touched his lips to hers. Yes, she thought, yes, yes, yes. . . .

WHAT ARE *LOVESWEPT* ROMANCES?

They are stories of true romance and touching emotion. We believe those two very important ingredients are constants in our highly sensual and very believable stories in the *LOVESWEPT* line. Our goal is to give you, the reader, stories of consistently high quality that may sometimes make you laugh, sometimes make you cry, but are always fresh and creative and contain many delightful surprises within their pages.

Most romance fans read an enormous number of books. Those they truly love, they keep. Others may be traded with friends and soon forgotten. We hope that each *LOVESWEPT* romance will be a treasure—a "keeper." We will always try to publish

*LOVE STORIES YOU'LL NEVER FORGET
BY AUTHORS YOU'LL ALWAYS REMEMBER*

The Editors

LOVESWEPT® • 369

Joan Elliott Pickart
The Magic of the Moon

BANTAM BOOKS
NEW YORK • TORONTO • LONDON • SYDNEY • AUCKLAND

THE MAGIC OF THE MOON

A Bantam Book / December 1989

*LOVESWEPT® and the wave device are registered
trademarks of Bantam Books, a division of
Bantam Doubleday Dell Publishing Group, Inc.
Registered in U.S. Patent
and Trademark Office and elsewhere.*

*If you would be interested in receiving protective vinyl
covers for your Loveswept books, please write to this address
for information:*

Loveswept
Bantam Books
P.O. Box 985
Hicksville, NY 11802

ISBN 0-553-44006-3

Published simultaneously in the United States and Canada

*Bantam Books are published by Bantam Books, a division
of Bantam Doubleday Dell Publishing Group, Inc. Its trademark, consisting of the words "Bantam Books" and the
portrayal of a rooster, is Registered in U.S. Patent and
Trademark Office and in other countries. Marca Registrada.
Bantam Books, 666 Fifth Avenue, New York, New York 10103.*

PRINTED IN THE UNITED STATES OF AMERICA

O   0 9 8 7 6 5 4 3 2 1

For Kay and Dana
Merry Christmas!

Prologue

Declan Harris pressed his fists into the small of his back as he straightened on the stool and twisted from side to side. He winced as the tightly coiled muscles protested.

He abandoned his attempts with a sigh, crossed his arms on top of his drafting table, and stared out the window. A vibrant summer sunset was streaking across the California sky in a breathtaking blend of purple, orange, yellow, and pink.

How many people, Declan mused, who were rushing to their homes in this affluent section of Los Angeles would notice the vibrant spectacle? Not many, he figured. He himself wouldn't have consciously stopped his work to view the sunset, set aside precious minutes to absorb nature's gift, because he didn't have a few minutes to spare. Not today, or yesterday, or in the days to come.

When had it begun, he wondered, this frantic race against time? This feeling that each day didn't hold enough hours to accomplish all that needed to be done? When had his priorities begun to shift, finally resulting in his focus being almost entirely on his work, the other areas of his life pushed into shadowy corners? How long had it been since he'd stopped with the sole purpose of doing nothing more than enjoying a sunset?

Lord, Declan thought, shaking his head in disgust, if anyone could read his mind, they'd be convinced he was feeling sorry for himself, and that was definitely not true. He worked hard by choice, pushing himself to the limit to achieve the goals he'd set for himself long ago. Those goals were a reality, because Harris and Cooper, Architects, had arrived.

Except there was no Cooper. Jeff was gone, had been in his grave for almost two years.

"Working late again, I see," a voice said.

Declan jerked in surprise and turned to see a man standing in the dimly lit hall beyond his open door. For a fleeting moment the shadowy figure was so startlingly familiar, it seemed to have been conjured by his memories of Jeff. Then the man stepped into the lighted office, and Declan let out a pent-up breath, chiding himself for his own foolishness.

"Hello, Bill," Declan said to the gray-haired man. "Yes, I'm here, but the real question is, why are you here? You're supposed to be semiretired, remember? You should be home by now."

The man walked slowly across the plushly furnished office to stare out the floor-to-ceiling window. The last streaks of the sunset were fading, the colors running together like melted butter.

"This city," Bill said, turning to look at Declan, "marches to a different drummer at night, one who brings out the evil in man, plays on the weaknesses of the innocent by offering things people shouldn't have. It . . ." He paused. "Enough. You don't need to hear me preach from my soapbox."

"I understand what you're saying, Bill, but you have to be fair. I go out into that night, just as you do. Each man makes his own choices. Jeff was drinking heavily the night he died and was driving his sports car far above the speed limit along that coast road. No invisible force pushed him and Suzanne Fairchild over that cliff."

"My son, Declan, is dead." Bill sighed. "Sometimes I still can't believe it. If he had become a doctor as we'd planned years ago, come into my practice and taken on the responsibilities of caring for human lives, he wouldn't have been so destructive with his own. I know, I know." He raised one hand. "Jeff told me a long time ago he didn't intend to follow in my footsteps, but I believe to this very day that if he had, he'd still be alive."

"You can't be positive of that. Look, why don't we change the subject? Running through a list of maybes and if onlys isn't going to bring Jeff back."

"You're right, and I apologize. I don't often become maudlin like this, filled with self-pity over the loss of my only child. Thanks to you, I have a purpose to my life. I focused on Jeff after my wife died when Jeff was small. Then . . . well, I saw no point in continuing to practice medicine after his death. What good is a legacy if there's no one to pass it on to? But you snapped me out of that over a year ago."

"Yep," Declan said, getting off the stool. He rotated his neck back and forth in an attempt to loosen the painfully tight muscles. "Want some coffee?"

"No, thanks. I came here to give you a report that troubles me."

"Oh?" Declan crossed the room to pour himself a mug of coffee, then turned and leaned back against the small bar.

"As you well know, I'm the company doctor, per se, for six firms in this building. You have fifteen people at Harris and Cooper now, and all of them passed their annual physicals last week with flying colors. Except for one of your top people."

"Really?" Declan took a swallow of coffee, then set the mug on the bar. "Who are you talking about? What's wrong with him, or her?"

"Humor me. Just listen to facts without a name. It's too easy to rationalize cause and effect when you know the personality involved. This is a man, age thirty-five, six feet tall, about one hundred and eighty pounds, excellent muscle tone, no excess weight. Doesn't smoke, doesn't drink to excess. However, he's showing signs of extreme fatigue and stress."

Declan pushed himself away from the bar and crossed his arms over his chest. "Go right ahead, Bill," he said, narrowing his eyes. "Tell me all about . . . myself."

"I should have held back on the description," Bill said. "Now you're defensive. Declan, I *am* talking about you. To use the modern slang, you are stressed out. You're already suffering from muscle tension, recurring headaches, inability to relax enough to sleep properly. You eat on the run, exist on caffeine jolts and sugar highs. You're starting to pop antacid tablets because your stomach is rebelling against the abuse. You haven't taken a day off in months and haven't even been to your health club for a workout in weeks. You're in trouble, Declan, and it's time to do something about it."

"Come off it, Bill," Declan said, his voice rising. "I never told you about my headaches. I breezed through that physical and you know it."

"You're right. Except for slightly high blood pressure, you checked out fine. But I saw the tension brewing in you. That's why I took you to lunch after your physical. We had a nice chat, if you recall."

"You set me up. I took a couple of aspirin while we

were eating and . . . Dammit, you really did a number on me."

"Your temper fuse is very short too. That's another sign of stress. I'm not playing games with you, Declan. Your body is screaming for mercy, and you'd better pay attention. Being young and healthy doesn't make you immune to serious repercussions from the way you're abusing yourself."

Declan opened his mouth to reply with an angry retort, then hesitated. He walked to the window, staring blindly at the congested traffic inching along the street ten floors below, then slowly turned to face Bill again.

"Okay," he said, "so I've been pushing. This company is growing in size and reputation, Bill, and it's not doing it on its own. It's up to me to see that we maintain the level of excellence we've become known for. It's my responsibility, no one else's."

"You hire only the best people, but you don't trust them to follow through. You don't delegate a thing. And you refuse to take on another partner. The level of stress you're subjecting yourself to can kill you, Declan. There it is, bottom line."

Declan shoved his hands into his pockets and stared up at the ceiling for a moment, aware that his temper was at a raw edge, and his head was pounding like a bongo drum.

"All right," he said at last. "You're a dirty player, Bill, but you won this hand. What do you want me to do?"

Bill took a business card from his jacket pocket. "This doctor is a psychologist who specializes in stress management."

"Whoa," Declan said, raising one hand. "Now you're going too far. I don't need a shrink to tell me I have to lighten up."

"I'm not asking you to become an official patient. Go after office hours tomorrow and have a friendly chat. Please, Declan, do this for me as well as for yourself."

Declan snatched the card out of Bill's hand. "Hell, all right, I'll go. You're a pain in the butt sometimes. Go away, I've got work to do."

"I'll leave you to your madness," Bill said, starting toward the door, "knowing these nights of your burning the midnight oil are drawing to a close." He stopped at the doorway. "I almost forgot to tell you. I had a call from that detective friend of yours. The one who handled Mildred Fairchild's case."

"I'm glad Vince Santini is back in this country after all those months in Italy." Declan paused. "Mildred Fairchild is the mother of the girl who was in the car with Jeff, right?"

"Yes. And you know, of course, that she had a mental breakdown when Suzanne died. She threatened to kill you, me, the bartender who served Jeff that night, Vince Santini, and a slew of other people. She's been in a sanitarium since the accident."

"Yes, I'm aware of that."

"Well, she was released yesterday with a clean bill of health. Vince called me when he couldn't reach you and said they have to take the doctor's word for it that she's no longer dangerous, but that we had the right to know that she wasn't safely tucked away. I said I'd pass the news on to you. I have to believe that the doctors at the sanitarium know what they're doing. Good night, Declan."

As Bill Cooper left his office, Declan glanced at the card in his hand, then did a quick double take.

"Hey!" he yelled. "Cooper, you reprobate, come back here. You didn't tell me you were shipping me off for a friendly chat with a *woman* shrink!"

He glared at the card. Dr. Joy Barlow—Psychologist. Hell. He didn't need some snooty woman telling him to cut back on his work load and coffee intake. And he'd make that very clear to Dr. Joy Barlow within the first ten minutes that he saw her.

In fact, ten minutes was just about how long this *one* get-together was going to last.

"And that," Declan said, shoving the card into his pocket, "is that."

One

Joy Barlow left her office and walked down the short hall to the reception area. Decorated in soft hues of burgundy and blue, the room was furnished with several comfortable chairs and two small tables on one side, and a desk on the other. A thin man in his late twenties, with sandy-colored hair and wearing wire-rimmed glasses, sat behind the desk. His fingers seemed to fly over the keys of his typewriter as he typed copy from papers spread out on the desk. He stopped typing and smiled at Joy as she approached.

"Here's Mrs. Mattingly's file, James," she said, dropping it into the "in" basket.

"Are your notes inside ready to be typed?" James asked.

"Yes," Joy said, smiling, "my chicken scratchings are there. It still amazes me that you can decipher my handwriting."

"It's grim, all right," James said. "Put that together with the fact that you're orthographically impaired, and we'll no doubt reach the mutually agreed-upon conclusion that I deserve a raise."

Joy laughed. "Orthographically impaired? I love it. The next time I'm at a party and some jerk makes a move on me, I'll look him right in the eye and say, 'Proceed at your own risk, buster. I'm orthographically impaired.' It sounds like a terrible social disease, and it has much more of a punch than announcing that I'm a lousy speller." She paused. "You just got a raise a month ago."

"I did? Me?" James said, splaying one hand on his chest. "Why, so I did. It slipped my mind, I guess."

"Nice try, James, but no cigar. It's time for you to call it a day. I have to stay here to meet with Declan Harris."

"A new patient? You didn't tell me to make up a file for him."

"No, not a patient. We have a mutual friend in Dr. Bill Cooper, and Mr. Harris and I are to meet, according to Bill, for a friendly chat regarding Mr. Harris's stress level. Bill set it up. It's obvious from what he said that Mr. Harris is not happy about talking with me. Well, I'm not thrilled about it, either. Under different circumstances I'd flatly refuse to see the recalcitrant Mr. Harris. It would seem that both of us are doing this because we're so fond of Bill. At least Declan Harris won't be a patient storming the gates on a regular basis."

" 'Tis not a pretty picture you paint, wise and wonderful Dr. Barlow. Actual patient or not, anyone here against his will is a pain in the katush."

"Politely put," Joy said with a sigh. "Well, I'll see you tomorrow."

"Ma'am," James called as she started away. "I'm going to finish this file before I leave, ma'am."

"Cut the 'ma'am,' James," Joy said over her shoulder. "You just had a raise, remember?"

"A guy has to try . . . ma'am."

Laughing softly, Joy reentered her office and glanced around, appreciating as always the welcoming atmosphere she'd created. She'd used the same hues of burgundy and blue as in the reception area, and the furnishings were of dark wood.

A sofa was against one wall, a coffee table in front of it, and matching tables at either end. Sunshine poured in through the large window behind her desk. Two easy chairs sat in front of the desk, near the lighted fish tank that was built into a paneled wall. Several species of tropical fish swam lazily back and forth in the tank.

Joy wandered across the room, enjoying the cushion of thick carpet, and stood before the massive fish tank. It was flush with the wall, and barely discernible lines in the paneling marked the place where doors could be opened to enable her to feed the fish and tend to the upkeep of the tank.

"Hi, guys," she said, tapping one finger on the tank. "How are things in Atlantis?"

Declan read the now-too-familiar name on the solid wood door and frowned. Dr. Joy Barlow, Psychologist. Great. He'd rather be at the dentist, and he really hated going to the dentist. The good doctor must charge outrageous hourly rates, judging from her Wilshire Boulevard address and what he'd seen so far of the building. The lobby was elegantly and expensively decorated, and the elevator that had whisked him up to the sixth floor was paneled in smoky, gold-veined mirrors.

He'd discovered, as he'd read the directory in the lobby, that lawyers, accountants, psychologists, and psychiatrists, as well as other professionals, had offices in the building. He figured they all charged exorbitant rates in order to afford the rent.

But, he decided sullenly, since Harris and Cooper hadn't designed the building, the whole thing would probably fall down within a year.

Now that, he admitted to himself, was a rotten,

nasty thought. It did, however, fit his mood perfectly. He was in a nasty, rotten frame of mind. Ten minutes. Maximum. That was going to be the length of his encounter with Joy Barlow.

He opened the door and entered the office, immediately glancing around and placing mental price tags on the obviously expensive furnishings. His scrutiny ended when his gaze landed on a young man sitting behind a desk.

"May I help you?" the bespectacled man said.

Declan slowly crossed the room to stand in front of the desk. "Declan Harris," he said gruffly. "Who are you?"

"James. I'm Dr. Barlow's secretary."

"You're her secretary? Why?"

"Why? Well, because I'm very good at what I do, and I enjoy this type of work. If you'll have a seat, Mr. Harris, I'll inform Dr. Barlow that you're here." James reached out one hand toward the telephone.

"Hold it," Declan said. "What's she like, this Dr. Barlow? Snooty, right? One of those I'm-smarter-than-you-are-and-don't-you-forget-it types, right? A feminist for sure. Having a guy for a secretary is a statement of superiority over the male sex. Terrific. Make that eight minutes, not ten."

"Pardon me?" James said.

"Forget it. Let's get this over with. I'm a busy man."

"Yes, sir." James lifted the receiver and pressed a button.

Joy picked up her telephone in her office. "Yes?"

"Mr. Harris is here," James said into the receiver.

"Is he hostile?"

"I've confirmed that, yes."

"Well, I'll be brave, courageous, and bold," Joy said. "Show Mr. Harris into my office, James."

"Yes, ma'am." He replaced the receiver and stood up. "Mr. Harris? If you'll follow me please."

Declan turned from the painting he was studying. "What? Oh, sure."

Barlow charged *really* outrageous hourly fees, he decided as he trailed behind James. That oil painting was an original. Half of her patients were probably bored society women who thought it sounded trendy to talk about their analyst as they sipped margaritas at the country club after a set of tennis. What a farce all of this was. He was cutting this nonsense down to six minutes.

James opened a door and stepped back. "Here you are, Mr. Harris."

"Thanks, kid," Declan said. That had an authentic, surly ring to it, he thought. The "kid" was probably only five or six years younger than he himself, but if Barlow had heard that, she'd be alerted to the fact that Declan Harris was not in a chipper mood.

Declan entered the office and heard the door close

behind him as his attention was immediately caught by the enormous fish tank on the far wall.

Oh, say now, he thought, that was classy. Whoever had designed the wall to encase the tank had done a helluva good job. The effect was striking, very—

"Hello, Mr. Harris."

Declan snapped his head around at the sound of the soft, feminine voice. In a sweeping glance he scrutinized, and memorized, every inch of the woman standing beside the desk. Unexpected heat rocketed through his body, and his heart started beating wildly.

One thought hammered against his brain. This was not what a psychologist was supposed to look like.

Dr. Joy Barlow, he thought incredulously, was beautiful. Absolutely beautiful. She was tall and slender, her delicate face dominated by big brown eyes. Her blond hair was swept back and secured at the base of her neck. How long was that hair when set free, he wondered.

His gaze dropped from her face, and he saw her figure was perfect. Full breasts, small waist, and very long, satiny legs.

She was wearing a flared white skirt, a wide black belt, and a long-sleeved silky black blouse with small white polka dots. Two ropes of white beads fell nearly to the top of the belt buckle.

And to think he'd wasted the word *classy* on a fish tank.

Standing before him was a very classy, stunning woman.

The heat that had shot through him when he'd first looked at Joy Barlow was now coiling low within him. He couldn't remember ever having such an instant, sensual response to a woman as he was having to Joy.

"Mr. Harris?" she said. "Would you care to have a seat?"

He nodded and walked forward to sit in one of the chairs in front of the desk.

Joy turned and retreated to the butter-soft leather chair behind her desk. Why had she done that? she asked herself. Her usual procedure was to shake the hand of the new patient in *front* of the desk, then slowly return to her chair until she could determine where to sit to make the person most at ease. Declan Harris wasn't even a patient, and there certainly was no reason for her to sit in a position of power.

So why on earth had she done that? As he had advanced, she had backed away, like a skittish animal being stalked by a large, determined cat. He was, without a doubt, one of the most handsome, blatantly masculine men she'd ever seen.

He was tall, with broad shoulders and a wide chest that tapered to narrow hips. His long legs were obviously muscular, despite being encased in tailored gray slacks. His green shirt matched his eyes perfectly, and he wore a gray-and-green paisley print tie. She guessed his gray suit coat was custom-tailored to accommodate those wide shoulders.

And his face. Deeply tanned, its rough-hewn features hadn't a hint of pretty-boy smoothness. He had a straight nose, square jaw, and the most gorgeous head of thick, inky black hair she'd ever had the pleasure of feasting her eyes on.

And his lips. How could a man with such chiseled-in-stone features have such soft, sensuous, kissable lips?

Was that the sound of her racing heart echoing in her ears, she wondered. This never happened to her. She never responded to a man, a stranger, on a purely lustful level. But, oh Lord, she wished someone would remind her body of that. Declan Harris was throwing her totally off kilter, and the heat pulsing throughout her gave evidence to that fact.

"So!" she said, a trifle too enthusiastically. "We have a mutual friend in Dr. Cooper."

Declan propped the ankle of one leg onto his other knee. "So it would seem." He really liked her voice. It was rich and husky. Imagine that voice whispering his name in the throes of passion. "Bill Cooper's son, Jeff, was my partner before he was killed two years ago."

"Jeff and I often played together as children, but I hadn't seen him for several years before he died. Dr.

Cooper and my father have been close friends ever since they were in medical school together. Bill was completely devastated by Jeff's death."

"Yes, I know. How long is your hair?"

She blinked. "I beg your pardon?"

Declan rested his elbows on the arms of the chair and made a steeple of his fingers. "Your hair. I was wondering how long it is."

She sat up straighter. "That's none of your concern, Mr. Harris. Shall we get down to business?"

"It's Declan." He gave her a slow, lazy grin. "I'd be more than happy to get down to . . . business, Doctor, but since I'm not a patient, why don't we go someplace for dinner? We can talk, get to know each other. Oh, and we should touch on the subject of stress for a couple of minutes in all fairness to Bill. All right?"

Oh, it shouldn't be legal, Joy thought. Declan Harris shouldn't have a sexy, knock-'em-dead smile and straight white teeth, on top of everything else he'd been dished out. Definitely against the law.

Go out to dinner with him? To what might be a cozy, romantic restaurant? No, not smart. Her sensual reactions to Declan were unsettling, to say the least, and not one bit welcome. She was accustomed to deciding herself on what plane she would interact with a given man. Declan was, somehow, pushing sexual buttons within her she hadn't even known existed.

"Thank you, but no," she said, looking somewhere over his right shoulder. "I don't care to go out to dinner. As you stated, in all fairness to Bill we should discuss the purpose for your being here. He told me that you're suffering from fatigue and extreme stress."

"Nothing I can't handle. I wish you'd reconsider about dinner." Damn, now he was stuck, he thought. If Joy wouldn't go out to dinner, he'd have to sit there with a massive desk separating them, because he had no intention of leaving yet. Joy Barlow was a beautiful, intriguing woman, and he most definitely wanted to spend some time with her. But he sure didn't want to have a strictly clinical discourse about his stress, for pete's sake. He'd steer her away from that subject. "I really like your fish tank. Who designed the placement of it in the wall?"

"I did. Mr. Harris—"

"Declan."

"All right, Declan, you don't seem to realize how dangerous stress can be. It has the potential to kill. Unfortunately, most people are unaware of the effects stress can have on their mind and body. I specialize in stress management, with programs tailored to meet each individual's needs."

"Good for you. You really designed the fish tank wall? I'm impressed. Did you copyright the design, or could I use it?"

Joy clenched her teeth as she gathered her patience, then plastered a phony smile on her face.

Not only was Declan causing her difficulties on a woman-to-man level, she thought, he was also threatening her professional demeanor. She'd been a breath away from yelling at him to stop avoiding the issue of his stress and listen to what she had to say. The mental image of sitting there in her office *yelling* was horrifying. Declan Harris was a menace.

"Declan," she said, still forcing a smile, "for Bill Cooper's sake, if not your own, let's try to accomplish something, shall we? He's very concerned about you. You seem to be doing everything you possibly can to avoid talking about your stress. Why?"

Declan was about to turn her question aside, but didn't. He looked at Joy for a long moment, then dropped his foot to the floor and leaned forward, a frown knitting his dark brows together.

"You're right," he said. "I don't want to address that subject. I'm angry, I suppose, because Bill hit the nail on the head, and I didn't want to hear it. I don't have time to hear it, don't have time to change how I'm living my life. Later, maybe, but not now. I came here to placate Bill, get him off my back for a while. Then when I met you I decided I'd really like to get to know you better . . . as corny as that sounds. Well, I sure blew this straight to hell." His hands on his thighs, he pushed himself to his feet. "I'll get out of your way."

"Don't go," Joy said. "Declan, don't do this to yourself. Stress management isn't that difficult once you get the hang of it. Is your work more important than your health, maybe even your life? Would you please stop and think about it for a minute?"

As Declan looked directly into Joy's big brown eyes, he felt a fleeting emotion that was gone before he could even identify it. Heat once again churned deep and heavy within him, and he was powerless to tear his gaze from Joy's.

There'd been such a pleading tone to her voice, he thought, as she'd asked him not to leave, as though she really cared what happened to him. A trick of the trade? A little psychological warfare perfected with long practice? Make the patient feel important, special; give the impression he was cared about on a personal level? Sure, that was it. The doctor had spoken, not the woman. And for some unknown reason he was disappointed.

"Do you need a few more patients to help pay the rent on this place?" he asked tightly.

Damn him, Joy thought. She pulled her gaze from his and stared at her hands, which were clutched tightly together on the top of the desk.

When she'd literally begged Declan to stay, to heed his body's signals and to protect himself from possible physical and mental harm, her words had come from a place within her that had nothing to do with her being a psychologist. Joy, the woman, had spoken.

Why had that happened? What was it about Declan

Harris that had caused her to lose her professional-ism? She'd felt the stirrings of desire deep within her and, held immobile under his compelling gaze, had pleaded with him not to go.

Oh, Lord, this was frightening.

She turned her head to see Declan staring into the fish tank, his profile to her. His jacket was swept back by his large hands planted on lean hips. A shiver coursed through her.

"I shouldn't have said that," he began quietly, continuing to stare into the fish tank. "About your needing more patients to pay the rent. I apologize. I realize that as a doctor it's your duty to do all you can to see that people receive the help they need." And the woman, he wondered. Had any of what she'd said been spoken by Joy, the woman? "Doctors are supposed to do that." He turned slowly to look at her. "Right?"

"Yes," Joy said, nodding, "but . . ." He didn't know, she thought, that she'd spoken as a woman, not a psychologist. Thank heavens for that much, at least. She was shaken to the core by her performance, but Declan was unaware of it. Her pride was intact.

"But?" he prompted.

"Nothing."

Damn, Declan thought. He'd hoped she was going to say more, admit that what she had said hadn't been a practiced clinical plea used on reluctant patients a hundred times in the past. Why did it matter so much? He really didn't know.

He lifted one hand and absently rubbed his fingertips back and forth over his forehead.

"Headache?" Joy asked.

He quickly dropped his hand.

"I know your symptoms, Declan, because Bill told me. You are definitely suffering from extreme stress. Your body is letting you know it's reached the saturation point as far as your abuse is concerned. You have a choice to make now; the ball is in your court. You can go blissfully on your way and pretend you're invincible until you pay the piper. Or you can take advantage of the resources available to you and correct a situation that is rapidly becoming completely out of control. It's up to you, Declan."

"Yes, it is, isn't it?" he said, and turned once again to stare into the fish tank.

What had happened to his vow to limit his appointment to ten minutes, reduced to eight, reduced to six? Joy Barlow had happened.

He shoved his hands into his trouser pockets, his fingers curling automatically around the tin of aspirin in one pocket and the roll of antacids in the other.

So, okay, he reasoned, those items were becoming integral parts of his life, and he always needed to be sure that they were in ample supply and within reach. But that was the way things were now. In the future he'd be able to slow down, work a normal number of hours each day. Later, somewhere down the road. But if he refused to cooperate with Joy, she'd show him the door. Guaranteed. But that wasn't going to happen. *He* would decide if he'd stay or go. This situation just called for a little ingenuity.

He pulled the aspirin and antacids out of his pockets and tossed them onto Joy's desk.

"I give up. I'm waving the white flag." He looked at her. "I'm all yours, Dr. Barlow."

Joy's heart did a funny little flip-flop at Declan's choice of words, but she decided to ignore it. She could not, however, stop her smile.

She got to her feet. "You've decided? You're going to take control of your life, follow the stress management program?"

Declan looked at her, glanced quickly at the tins of tablets on the desk, then met her gaze again. "Yes. I'm not thrilled about this, you understand, but . . . yes."

Joy walked around the edge of the desk. "Oh, Declan, I'm so glad." She looked directly into his green eyes, and her smile faded. "I . . . really am."

Declan felt his body tighten as he continued to look at Joy. "Why?" he asked, his voice raspy.

"Because I . . ." Because she didn't want anything to happen to him. Because she couldn't think straight when he looked at her like that. Because . . . oh, darn it, just because.

He lifted a hand and drew his thumb lightly over her lips. "You have," he said, stepping closer to her, "the most kissable lips I have ever seen." He slowly lowered his head to hers. "I'm going to go crazy if I don't kiss you, Joy Barlow."

No! her mind yelled. "Oh," was all she managed to say.

Declan cradled her face in both hands and kissed her.

Yes! Joy thought, her lashes drifting down. His lips were even softer, more sensuous, than she'd imagined.

Heated desire curled and swirled within her. Declan's tongue parted her lips in gentle insistence, and she complied, meeting his tongue eagerly with her own.

She'd been waiting for this kiss. An hour? A day? A lifetime? She didn't know, it didn't matter, because it was happening now, and it was like no kiss before.

Sweet nectar, Declan thought hazily. Joy tasted like sweet nectar. Her lips were custom-ordered just for him, and he'd been waiting forever to claim them. This kiss was heaven.

But this kiss was going to lead to a private hell if he didn't end it. Already his body was aching with the desire to have this exquisite woman.

He reluctantly lifted his head, his hands still framing her face. "I have to stop, Joy," he said huskily. "For now. You're turning me inside out, Doctor."

Doctor? Joy thought dreamily. Who? Oh, good Lord.

Her eyes popped open, then widened in horror. She took a quick step backward, forcing Declan to release her. Her own hands flew to her flushed cheeks.

"What am I doing? What have I done?"

Declan frowned. "Hey, we shared a sensational kiss, not a quickie on the top of your desk. Don't get so shook up."

"I can't kiss you."

He grinned at her. "You sure fooled me. That was one hell of a kiss, Dr. Barlow."

"Which never should have happened." She returned to her chair, her trembling legs refusing to support her for another moment as she sank onto the soft leather. "I can't believe I did that."

"Trust me, you did," he said, still smiling. "My libido will sign an affidavit testifying to the fact. Joy, come on. You're overreacting. It was a kiss. A fantastic one, yes, but not enough to get us arrested."

"You don't understand, Declan. I'm a doctor, you're my patient. I have a level of professionalism to maintain here. I have never in my entire career done anything so . . . Maybe you should see someone else who specializes in stress management."

"Whoa," he said, lifting a hand. "First, I'm not your patient. Granted, you shouldn't help me for free, so we'll exchange services. I'll design a house for you or something. How's that? I'm not signing up for set appointments with a psychologist, Joy. Not a chance."

He most certainly did have to have scheduled appointments, she thought indignantly. Then she heard herself say, "That's fine. No scheduled appointments. However, you must understand that from here on out we will maintain professional attitudes. I apologize for my behavior and assure you that it positively won't happen again."

"Now that," he said, chuckling, "was snooty."

"Declan!"

"Okay, okay." He quickly raised both hands. "No problem. We'll take it one step at a time. You're going to unstress me. Where do we start?"

"I'd like you to carry a small notebook with you wherever you go for the next three days. Jot down what you are doing at the beginning of each hour. I'll get in touch with you on Friday."

"Check."

"Also, starting today you're to set aside an hour a day to exercise."

His grin slid back into place. "Interesting. What kind of exercise do you recommend? Outdoor or . . . indoor? *Hmm?*"

Joy gritted her teeth. "Do you belong to a health club, Mr. Harris?"

"Yep."

"Then work out there for an hour a day," she said, her voice ringing with false sweetness.

"Got it. Are you positive that you're not suffering from a dab of stress yourself, Doctor? You seem a bit uptight." He picked up the aspirin tin and ant-acid tablets and set them squarely in front of her. "There. We'll share." He leaned over and dropped a quick kiss on her lips. "Just like we shared the kiss." He straightened and started toward the door. "Talk to you soon, Joy. We're in this together now." He left the office, closing the door behind him.

"We're in this together now," Joy repeated weakly, waving a hand breezily in the air. "Good heavens, what has that man done to me?"

Two

Joy stepped out of the house and onto the patio and was greeted by the wildly thumping tail of a large nondescript dog. The dog lifted his head, but didn't get to his feet.

She grinned. "Hello, Butch. Lazy as ever, I see."

A man who was stretched out in a lounge chair turned his head and smiled at Joy. "Ah, the great psychologist comes to visit her father. You notice that I didn't get up, either. Butch and I have this retirement business down to an art, and we're enjoying every minute of it. Does Janie know you're here? She'll want to feed you some dinner."

"I saw her and actually convinced her I didn't need a thing. She's been trying to fatten me up since I was twelve."

"She's a good soul. Lord knows how we would have survived without her after your mother died. Sit, Dr. Barlow, and tell me why you look like the weight of the world is on your shoulders."

Joy sighed and sat in a cushioned lawn chair. "You know me too well, Dr. Barlow."

"I love you, and there can never be too much of that. What's wrong, Joy?"

"Nothing. Everything. Oh, I don't know." She shook her head, then sighed again. "A doctor's office is sacred, right? Of course it is. When one is there dealing with a patient, one must conduct oneself with strict professionalism. Anything less is unbecoming to my title, my oath, my reputation. Well, not that he's a patient but . . . no, he isn't a patient, so why am I so shook up?"

"I wondered where all this was going," Jack Barlow said with a chuckle. "So there's a "he" involved. Unbecoming to your title, oath, and reputation? That certainly sounds snooty. When did you become so snooty?"

"Snooty! That's what he said after I said there would be no more . . . no more of what there had been." She cleared her throat and shifted uncomfortably. "I am *not* snooty."

"Oh, I don't know about that. Apparently the vote is running two to one for snooty at the moment."

"Would you stop that? This is serious. It's disgraceful. I'm very upset by what happened."

"Lord above, child, what did you do? Dance naked with the guy on your desktop?"

"Jack Barlow, that's sick. I kissed him, that's all. No, he kissed me. Well, actually, we kissed each other." She threw up her hands. "It just never should have happened."

"He's a lousy kisser, huh?"

"Oh, no, no," she said, a sudden dreamy quality to her voice. "It was wonderful. I have never felt so . . ." She blinked. "Darn it, Dad, you're not helping me one little bit."

"Oh, honey, what can I say? Whoever this man is, he obviously had an impact on you. Can't you just relax a bit, wait and see what happens in the natural order of things?"

"The way I reacted to him was not natural," Joy said, with a sniff of disgust.

"Wasn't it? I think perhaps it was. New and different for you, but very natural. When I met your mother, I knew I was experiencing something I'd never known before. The thing is, Joy, I didn't run from it or deny what I was feeling for Marilee. Quit frowning at me like that." He stroked his chin thoughtfully. "You know, I would suggest . . ."

"Yes?" Joy said, leaning forward.

"That you remember to lock your office door if you decide to dance naked on your desktop with the guy." Jack dissolved in a fit of laughter. Butch wagged his tail exuberantly.

Joy got to her feet. "Good-bye, sir. I'll write to you after they cart you away."

"Sit," Jack said, flapping a hand at her as he controlled his merriment. She sat. "Okay, let's get serious."

"Don't strain yourself," she said sullenly.

"Did you say that this man isn't your patient?"

"No, he isn't, not really. We've begun working on a stress-management program for him, but it's all unofficial. Bill Cooper sent him to me because Bill is very concerned about Declan's level of stress. Declan came to see me out of respect and friendship for Bill, and I agreed to meet with him for the same reasons."

"Declan?"

"Declan Harris. Jeff Cooper was his partner."

"Ah, I thought the name sounded familiar. It was Declan Harris who managed to pull Bill out of his black depression after Jeff was killed. I couldn't reach Bill, no one could. I was very afraid that he was even suicidal. Then Declan Harris convinced Bill to work part-time as a company physician on a preventive medicine program. I'd say that Declan Harris quite literally saved Bill's life."

"I had no idea. I knew that Bill was completely grief-stricken when Jeff was killed, but I didn't realize . . . Declan turned things around for Bill?"

Jack nodded. "Declan is obviously a very caring man."

"Yes," she said softly. She stared into space for a long moment, then shook her head as if clearing it and looked at her father again. "Declan is also stressed out to a potentially dangerous degree, Dad."

"So, Bill is stepping in and doing something about it, repaying the debt he owes Declan. Bill sent Declan to the finest stress-management specialist in town . . . my daughter, Joy Marilee Barlow."

"Thank you for the compliment, but said specialist kissed the socks off said stressed-out man," Joy said miserably, rolling her eyes heavenward.

"Quit being so hard on yourself. Declan isn't your patient. You're looking for trouble that simply isn't there. Methinks it's time for the ol' physician-heal-thyself number. You need to realize that you did nothing more than behave like a woman. I say, 'Hooray for you.' Am I getting through to you?"

"I don't know. I'm so confused right now, I could just scream. I want to crawl into bed and sleep for five years. I think I'll go home and treat myself to a long, leisurely bubble bath."

"Good therapy. Take a glass of wine into the tub with you. Pamper yourself for a change."

"I will." She stood, then leaned over to kiss her father on the cheek. "Thanks, Dad."

"You keep me posted on this, young lady."

"There may be nothing more to tell you. For all I know, Declan Harris forgot that kiss the moment he left my office. Good night, Dad."

"Well, Butch," Jack said as Joy left the patio, "how much are you betting that Declan Harris *didn't* forget that kiss when he walked out the door?"

Butch thumped his tail wildly.

Declan tossed the thin pencil onto the drafting board with an earthy expletive, slid off the stool, and began to pace the length of his large office.

Joy Barlow, he fumed, was driving him crazy. He was acting like an adolescent who had stolen a kiss behind the barn and was now starry-eyed over the girl. A kiss was a kiss, for cripe's sake.

But not when it was a kiss shared with Joy.

And it wasn't just pure male lust.

Declan stopped and stared into space. That truth, he admitted, was what was really gnawing at him like a persistent toothache. Strange and new emotions had surged through him when he'd captured Joy's mouth with his, felt the lush softness of her lips and the seductive stroking of her tongue as it dueled with his. And he could still taste her sweet nectar.

What in the name of heaven was Joy Barlow doing to him?

Declan muttered another expletive, then pushed back the cuff on his shirt to look at his watch. He should eat a decent dinner for a change, he supposed, and then go to the health club for his hour workout.

Why someone suffering from stress should sweat for an hour at a health club, torturing his muscles, he had no idea. It sounded crazy, but not putting in that hour of exercise would seem like lying to Joy.

He grabbed his suit coat off the back of a chair, smacked out the light over the drafting table, and headed for the door with heavy strides.

"You are really driving me nuts, Joy Barlow," he said to the empty room. "Right out of my ever lovin' mind."

Nearly three hours later Declan stepped out of the elevator on the fourteenth floor of the high-rise apartment building where he lived and shuffled down the hall.

He was, he knew without a flicker of a doubt, a dying man.

It had been too many weeks since he'd worked out at the club, and the hour he'd put in had seemed two centuries long. Even after an endless shower, using the hottest water he could stand, every muscle in his body was still screaming for mercy. At the moment Dr. Joy Barlow was not his favorite person. Should she suddenly appear in front of him, he'd be only too happy to tell her what she could do with her hour of exercise.

Declan entered his large apartment and immediately began to strip off his clothes, not bothering to turn on a light. The trail of discarded garments followed him into the bedroom, where he flipped back the sheets and crawled naked onto the bed.

Within moments he was deeply asleep before he could wonder if he'd spend another night tossing and turning as he'd done for the past several weeks.

"Good morning, James," Joy said.

"Hi. Coffee is made," James said, glancing up at her. "You look like you could use some."

"I didn't sleep too well last night. I had a lot on my mind. My own remedies for turning off the mental faucet didn't work, so . . . what does my day add up to?"

"Full. This is Wednesday, you know. You're scheduled to do the Vietnam vets group session this afternoon."

"Yes, of course."

"The files for your morning appointments are on your desk."

"Thank you."

In her office Joy poured the sought-after coffee into a mug, then settled behind her desk. She took a sip of what she hoped was going to be energizing brew and knew it wasn't going to work.

She was exhausted before her long day began, she thought gloomily. She couldn't have gotten more than three hours of sleep, even though the night had seemed to stretch on forever.

And it was all Declan Harris's fault!

Great, she thought dryly. Some psychologist she was. She was transferring the blame onto Declan for her own inability to control her mental processes.

But darn it, it was as though he'd been right there in her bedroom with her throughout the endless night. She'd heard his voice, his throaty chuckle, seen his smile and his gorgeous green eyes. Images of his magnificent body had taunted her.

And the kiss?

Over and over she'd relived that kiss, that incredible kiss. The one she hadn't wanted to end. The one that had evoked a desire within her that still smoldered like an ember waiting to be rekindled. The kiss that had stirred emotions as well as passion, emotions she didn't understand but that definitely unsettled her.

Oh, what an absolutely hideous night it had been.

It was a lucky thing for Mr. Harris, she decided, that he wasn't scheduled to see her today. She'd probably haul off and punch him right in the nose.

Joy took another swallow of coffee. Friday, she mused. D day. Declan day. Well, thank goodness, she had plenty of time between now and then to settle herself down, get back on her professional track.

She'd blown the episode with Declan totally out of proportion. By Friday she'd be one hundred percent in control.

Oh, what a relief. Everything was going to be fine.

As the day progressed, Joy began to doubt seriously that all would be well by the time she spoke with Declan again on Friday. He kept strutting into her mental vision, simply refusing to leave her alone.

"I'm back from lunch," James said from the doorway to her office.

"Fine," Joy said, getting to her feet. "I'm starving. Maybe food will . . . Never mind. Hold down the fort, James."

She left the office, pulling the door closed, then turned and bumped squarely into a very solidly built man.

"Excuse me, I—Declan!"

"Hi," he said, smiling at her. Hello, beautiful Joy, he thought. He'd decided that seeing her might push her image from his brain. "How about some lunch? Looks like my timing was perfect. You are going to lunch now, aren't you?"

"Well, yes, but . . ." Joy's voice trailed off. She wasn't prepared to see Declan today! Her heart was racing and her stomach felt strange. Good grief, this was insane. But perhaps it was better to move up the timetable, spend an hour with Declan now to get things back in their proper perspective. "I'd be delighted to go to lunch with you."

"You would? I mean, great. Let's go."

He grabbed her elbow and started toward the elevator, and she nearly had to run to keep up with him.

The restaurant that she suggested when he asked was a block from her office building and was fashioned after an English pub. They were seated at a table next to the windows that overlooked a small, grassy courtyard.

After ordering the fish and chips they both had decided on, Declan leaned back in his captain's chair and folded his arms loosely across his chest.

"I wrote in my notebook that I was going out to lunch," he said. "It made me realize it's been a long time since I left the office to eat lunch. I've been ordering in from a deli."

"And working while you eat," Joy said.

"Yes." He glanced around. "This is a nice place."

"It sounds to me like you've forgotten about nice places to eat, and enjoyable social events. Declan, have you ever asked yourself why you're working so hard, pushing the way you are?"

"Jeff and I set up goals for Harris and Cooper. The firm has achieved those goals, and we have an excellent reputation. Competition is stiff, though. I can't just sit back and let another outfit take our spot. Jeff used to work every bit as hard as I am."

"Jeff also used to play," she said quietly. "He had balance in his life."

Declan's jaw tightened. "Did he? Balance? I'm not

so sure about that, Joy. He was really living in the fast lane at the time he died. I don't know, it was as though he were trying to fill a void in his life. We didn't talk about it, but he'd definitely changed some of his values. But his work? Sensational. Always. He did more than his share to put Harris and Cooper on the map."

"I see," she said, looking at him intently. "So you're protecting Jeff's reputation as well as your own with this incredible work load of yours."

"Yes, I suppose I am," Declan said. "Ah, here's our lunch. It looks and smells terrific. I'm definitely coming here again."

She smiled. "Good. Relaxing lunches are an excellent way to unwind a bit in the middle of the day." She took a bite of fish. "Delicious. Did you exercise?"

He chuckled. "I suggest you don't press that issue at the moment. I exercised. Let it go at that."

"You'll put in another hour today, won't you?"

He looked up from his plate. "Yes, I'll do it. I slept like a rock."

She was glad someone had, she thought dryly. She'd been too busy herself chasing images of Declan through her mind. And she had a sneaky suspicion that having lunch with him wasn't going to solve her preoccupation-with-Declan Harris problem one iota.

Three

"Good night," James said, poking his head into Joy's office. "I'll see you tomorrow . . . good old Friday, TGIF, and all that rot. I've got to hustle because Thursday is my bowling night, and since I'm the star of the team, I can't be late. You don't look ready to go home. It is that time of day, you know."

"I'm going to stay awhile and get started on an article on stress management that I'm writing for one of the psychology publications."

"I read somewhere that California has been proved to be the undisputed stress capital of this country."

"I can believe that. Go bowl your little heart out, James. I'll see you in the morning."

"Okay, chief. Don't work too late. Bye."

"Good night, James."

A curtain of silence seemed to fall over the room, and Joy stared bleakly at the papers on her desk.

She was, she admitted, kidding herself if she actually thought she could concentrate right now on writing an article that would impress the community of psychologists across the country.

She knew, and detested the knowledge, that she was sitting there like a lump for the simple—no, complicated—reason that she didn't want to go home to her empty apartment.

Well, not quite empty, she thought, because Declan, drat the man, would trek right in the door with her and no doubt cause her to spend another night tossing and turning in her big bed. Having lunch with him the previous day had solved none of her confusion about him.

With a disgusted shake of her head and a dejected sigh tossed in for good measure, Joy leaned back in her chair and closed her eyes.

She had a headache, a painful throbbing that felt as if a couple of teenagers were beating on snare drums in her head. Her stomach hurt too, with a burning sensation that indicated she was in dire need of food. But she didn't want to move. She was listless, lethargic, as though she didn't have enough energy to budge an inch. A vague sense of depression seemed to be inching in around her and . . .

Joy sat bolt upright, her eyes wide. "Stress. I'm

suffering from symptoms of stress. I can't believe this."

She lunged forward and yanked open the center drawer of her desk to stare at the tin of aspirin and roll of antacid tablets Declan had left with her. Then she slammed the drawer closed and jumped to her feet, her mind racing. She had to nip this in the bud, start on a self-prescribed stress-reduction program at once. She'd go home and spend an hour on the lighted jogging track behind her apartment building. How long had it been since she'd exercised? She couldn't remember. Well, it didn't matter, because tonight she'd begin a regimented program.

She nodded decisively, then picked up her purse and started across the room, only to stop statue-still as she heard a strange noise in the outer office. A sudden blast of cold air swept over her, and she gasped in surprise, her gaze flying to the air-conditioning vent in her office. It was now spewing forth what felt like an arctic wind.

"Wonderful," she muttered. "The air-conditioning is acting up again."

With a wave of relief at knowing what had caused the noise in the reception area, she hurried from her office to the front. The magazines set out for waiting patients were strewn across the carpeting.

She set her purse on the floor and began to pick up the scattered magazines. A single page, which she figured had been torn out by the blast of air, caught her eye, and she glanced at it as she straightened.

"The Blue Moon," she read aloud.

After placing the magazines back where they belonged, Joy continued to read the brief article beneath a half-page picture of a full moon. The article stated that every decade or so a full moon appeared twice in one month. The first time was during the first couple of days of the month; the second during the last couple. The second full moon was called the blue moon.

Although, Joy read on, there was nothing mystical about the second full moon, a romantic legend had grown up around it. The Legend of the Blue Moon was that any man and woman who had chosen to be in each other's company and who witnessed the rising of the blue moon while together would fall irrevocably in love.

"Fancy that," Joy murmured.

She carefully folded the page and tucked it into her purse, wondering how long it had been since a blue moon had been seen. What a shame that the fairy-tale legend wasn't widely known so that the romantics of the world could enjoy it.

She turned off the lights and left the office, locking the door behind her. When she got home, she decided, she'd call the information hot line at the library and find out when the next blue moon was due to appear.

"The Legend of the Blue Moon," she said softly as she rode down in the elevator. "Oh, I adore it."

Joy slipped a pale blue cotton caftan over her head and reached for her hairbrush. She brushed her hair, braided it into a single plait, then coiled and pinned it into a loose figure eight at the back of her head.

She felt marvelous, she reaffirmed to herself as she left the bedroom. She'd had an invigorating run, then a hot shower. Now she'd eat a nourishing dinner and curl up with a good book. She'd recognized her stress for what it was, dealt with it, and was once more totally relaxed and calm. Splendid.

She was crossing her living room when a knock at the door caused her to stop so suddenly, she wobbled. Her eyes widened and she pressed one hand over her wildly beating heart.

"Oh, right," she muttered as she stomped to the door, "I'm really calm and relaxed. Ha!" She flung open the door, a glare firmly in place for whomever was on the other side. "Declan!"

Her scowl was replaced by an expression of shock at finding him standing there smiling at her, wearing jeans and a blue knit shirt. He looked marvelous in casual clothes, and what he did for jeans was close to sinful.

"Hello, Joy," he said. He lifted a brown paper bag to her eye level. "I have a problem."

"Oh?"

"Yep. It's chocolate chip ice cream that is beginning to melt and needs emergency attention." He raised his eyebrows. "As in two bowls and two spoons?" She looked sensational, he thought, young and carefree and smiling that lovely smile of hers. Her feet were bare. Nice feet. "Am I tempting you?"

If he only knew, Joy thought, her gaze sliding quickly over him once again. "Come in, Declan. Ice cream sounds like a perfect treat." She'd eat a nourishing dinner tomorrow night. "Did you exercise?" she asked as she closed the door.

Declan glanced around the apartment. The white wicker furniture with mint-green and yellow cushions created a bright, cheerful aura in the neat-as-a-pin room. There was a bookcase filled with books against one wall, and an expensive television and stereo system on another.

"Nice place," he said. "I like what you've done."

"Thank you. Shall we go serve up the ice cream?"

They took their dessert to an oak table in the dining alcove off the kitchen.

"*Mmm,*" Joy said, closing her eyes as the first bite of ice cream slid down her throat.

Declan chuckled, then took a bite of his. "Oh, yeah, this is the stuff. Jeff got me hooked on chocolate chip. Sometimes I really go for broke and have mint chocolate chip."

"Decadent," Joy said. "Actually, I can remember having chocolate chip ice cream with Jeff when we were kids. I guess he always liked it." She paused. "Declan, do you think Jeff would approve of your working to the point of neglecting other aspects of your life? You said that you're protecting his reputation as well as your own. The Jeff Cooper I knew would have called a halt to the pace you're maintaining."

"It won't always be like this," Declan said, frowning.

"Won't it? You're setting patterns that will be difficult to change. You'll begin to feel guilty when you're not working."

"Guilty?" His frown deepened. "I don't have anything to feel guilty about. Not in the present, the future, and especially the past."

"I didn't say—"

"Harris and Cooper is doing just fine. I owe that to Jeff, like a debt, because . . ." He stopped speaking for a moment. "Come on, Joy, let's lighten up and give this ice cream the attention it deserves."

"All right. I wish you'd finish your sentence, though. Why do you feel you owe Jeff?"

He shrugged. "It's not that big a deal. You're making too much out of an idle statement. We're changing the subject, remember?"

"Yes." She nodded. It *was* a big deal, she mused. She somehow knew it was. What was bothering

Declan about Jeff? Declan felt he *owed* it to Jeff to make a success of Harris and Cooper, but didn't want to discuss the reason. Why?

They finished their ice cream, rinsed the bowls, then wandered back into the living room. Declan began to examine Joy's choice of cassettes for the stereo.

"Pick something," she said, settling onto the sofa.

As she gazed at him, she realized he was filling the room to overflowing. She was aware of every inch of his magnificent body, could smell his aftershave and a lingering aroma of soap. She now saw that the tips of his hair were still damp from a shower he'd probably taken after working out. Declan was just so *there* all of a sudden, and her heart was beating a rapid tattoo.

Soft, dreamy music floated through the air.

Declan turned, his eyes meeting Joy's. Invisible threads seemed to pull at him, urging him to move, to close the distance between them. He walked slowly toward her, their gazes still locked in a mesmerizing hold.

"I'll put this in my notebook," he said, stopping in front of her. "I'll write down that I kissed, very thoroughly kissed, Joy Barlow"—he sat down next to her—"on the sofa in her living room. Right?"

"Oh, well, I . . ."

"Right, Joy?"

"Right," she said on a little puff of air.

He slid one hand to the nape of her neck and covered her lips with his, his tongue meeting hers in the sweet darkness of her mouth. She circled his neck with her arms as her eyes drifted closed. The kiss deepened, and the music played on.

Heat swept through Joy like a magical rushing brook, stealing her breath and flushing her cheeks.

How alive she felt, and feminine, and so very aware of the differences between man and woman, between Declan and herself. She'd never felt like this, never experienced such overwhelming desire intertwined with indefinable emotions.

A soft purr of pleasure caught in her throat.

Declan groaned when he heard the sensual sound. He lifted his head to take a needed breath, then his mouth melted over hers again. He dropped his hand from her neck and drew her close to him, wrapping his arms around her.

Heaven and hell, he thought foggily. Joy was heaven in his embrace, and his body ached with the want of her. The heat pounding through his veins was like marching soldiers from hell. He had to stop kissing her before he lost control. He had to stop kissing her *now*.

He raised his head, but made no attempt to speak, waiting for his breathing to slow. Joy opened her eyes and met his smoldering gaze.

At that instant the music stopped.

"That . . ." Declan started, then cleared his throat. "That is my cue to leave." He managed a slight smile. "Will I see you tomorrow? You said we'd touch base on Friday."

"Can you come to my office at four?"

"I'll be there." He brushed his lips over hers. "I'll let myself out. Good night, Joy."

"Good night, Declan."

She turned to watch him leave, then leaned her head back.

Tonight, she knew, would be spent tossing and turning again.

At nine o'clock the next morning Joy sank gratefully into the chair behind her desk and allowed the false smile she'd given James to fade.

If anyone knew, she thought dismally, that she'd hardly been able to get out of bed that morning because of the aching muscles in her legs, she'd be mortified. She could barely move. She had to think about something else besides her agony.

Declan.

No, she told herself, she was wearing out her brain thinking about Declan Harris. She was a befuddled mess thanks to him, and she was not going to dwell on him.

The Legend of the Blue Moon, she thought suddenly. Yes, of course, that was a wonderful topic.

She'd forgotten to call the library to see when the next blue moon was due to appear.

She retrieved the article from her purse, then took out the telephone book and flipped through the pages. The sore muscles in her legs were momentarily forgotten.

Declan stood in the corridor outside Joy's office and stared unseeingly at the nameplate on the wooden door. He was early for his four o'clock meeting, but he'd been worthless as far as accomplishing anything in his office. His concentration was blown, his thoughts already with Joy.

He'd never had a woman consume his thoughts the way Joy did. He was a wreck thanks to her, but he still wanted her like no woman before.

He frowned and entered the office.

"Good afternoon, Mr. Harris," James said pleasantly. "Dr. Barlow is expecting you. I won't escort you since you're not a patient."

"Fine."

He walked down the short hall to where Joy's office door was halfway open. He stepped inside the office and closed the door.

And then he saw Joy.

His heart thundered in his chest as he gazed at her. She stood facing him, the lighted fish tank with its tropical fish an intriguing backdrop behind her.

She was wearing a lightweight sweater striped diagonally in shades of blue, from royal to powder. Her blue skirt fit smoothly over her hips, then flared gently to below her knees. Her hair was twisted into its usual style at the nape of her neck, but her eyes looked bigger, browner, Declan thought hazily, and her lips actually seemed to be beckoning to him, urging him to claim them with his own.

Declan, Declan, Declan, Joy's mind hummed. He was there. At last he was there. The day had passed with agonizing slowness. Second by second, matched by each beat of her heart, she'd waited for this moment.

In a dark pin-striped suit, pristine white shirt, and dark tie, he was magnificent. His eyes were like emeralds, his thick dark hair like night itself. And his lips. Oh, how she remembered the feel and taste of those sensuous, soft lips.

Neither spoke as they gazed at each other. Currents of sensuality seemed to crackle between them as their hearts pounded and heat pulsed within them.

"Hell of a long day," Declan said.

"Yes," Joy whispered.

They moved at the same moment. Message sent; message received. No more words were necessary.

They met in the center of the room, Joy's arms floating upward to encircle Declan's neck, his wrapping around her, hands pressing against her back to pull her close.

He captured her lips, and she parted them to welcome his tongue that dueled and danced, exploring every crevice of her mouth.

The kiss was burning heat, and aching desire, and unquenchable hunger. The kiss was Joy and Declan, sharing all that they were.

Declan slid his hands down to Joy's buttocks and nestled her in the cradle of his hips. His arousal was straining against his slacks as tension built low and heavy within him. He drank of Joy's sweetness, savoring the feel of her breasts crushed to his chest, inhaling her aroma of spring flowers. He filled his senses with all of her as his body ached for the release that only she could bring him.

Joy trembled as she returned Declan's demanding kiss in total abandon. He felt so good, and smelled so good, and tasted so good, and her body was tingling with pure ecstasy. Such strength he possessed, and yet such gentleness. Desire thrummed within her as he ignited each of her senses to an almost painful awareness.

Oh, how she wanted this man, wanted to make love with Declan Harris.

He lifted his head and drew in a rough breath. His

lips still close to hers, he spoke in a voice gritty with passion. "Lord, how I want you. Can you feel it? My desire for you?"

"Yes," she whispered.

"I didn't come here with the intention of kissing you, Joy. What I mean is, I didn't sit in my office and plan this. It just happened."

"I didn't plan this, either, but I couldn't have stopped myself. Oh, Declan, this is all so confusing, and it frightens me because I don't seem to have control of myself around you. And I think about you when I'm not with you and . . . I don't know . . . It's very unsettling." She slowly drew her arms from his neck and took a small step backward. "Am I making any sense?"

"Most definitely," he said, smiling. "I've been rather jarred and jangled myself. I'm not sure what all of this means, Joy, but the thing is, I'm not positive that I want to know. I don't have time to devote to a serious relationship right now." He stared up at the ceiling for a moment, then met her gaze again. "Lord, that sounded cold. You're right, this is very confusing. A part of me knows I'm not ready for anything serious, but I can't seem to put you out of my mind for five minutes at a stretch. Actually, this situation is hell."

"Stressful," she said. "I know. When I realized that I was suffering from symptoms of stress I— What I mean is . . . oh, darn."

"You?" he said, raising his eyebrows. "The pro, the coach, the expert, is stressed out?"

"I didn't want you to know. It's embarrassing, really mortifying. A stress-management specialist who has stress. It's so terrible I can get a stress headache just thinking about it."

"Very interesting," Declan said, "but what I want to know is if you exercised."

"Could we sit down?" she asked, sweeping one hand toward the two easy chairs in front of her desk.

Declan nodded, then watched in fascination as Joy carefully eased herself onto one of the chairs. He settled in the other one and stared at her for a long moment.

"Why are you moving so . . ." he started, then whooped with laughter. "You *did* exercise. Your muscles hurt, right? Did you put in an hour, a full, agonizing, dying-in-the-morning hour?"

"This isn't funny, Declan. My legs are killing me. I ran for an hour last night just before you showed up with the ice cream. I'm miserable."

"Which should prove to you that exercising to relieve stress is dumb, Dr. Barlow."

"It certainly is not," she said indignantly. "I didn't make it up, you know. I don't prescribe exercise for lack of something to say."

"Pain isn't stressful? Come on, Doctor, give me a break."

"Declan, it has been scientifically proved that during high-stress times many physical changes take place within the body. Adrenaline floods your system, in addition to other chemicals, creating a sort of chemical traffic jam. Exercise produces peptides and other calming agents that help to fight and defuse stress."

"You're kidding. This exercise bit is for real?"

"Absolutely, and I resent the implication that you think I don't know what I'm doing in my profession. Do you believe that I'd be suffering like this if it wasn't going to pay off in the long run?"

"I'll be damned," he said, shaking his head. "I really thought it was some phony number to make the patient feel like he was doing something constructive about his stress. You know, like a sugar pill, a placebo."

"Well, thanks a lot. You're really getting insulting here. Exercise is very important. All kinds of things help stress. That fish tank isn't here just to look nice. The lazy back-and-forth motion of the fish has a calming effect on some people. Not everyone, but some. If I feel that a patient is responding to the fish, I recommend he get a small tank for his home."

"Fish?" Declan laughed. "This is nuts. What other off-the-wall stuff is relaxing?"

"The moon, Mr. Harris," she said stiffly. "Well, not the moon per se, but the idea of stopping to look at it, enjoying the beauty, the serenity of it. I'm doing that myself because I intend to see the blue moon."

"The who moon?"

"There's an article on my desk there that explains it. I'd get up and hand it to you, but my legs would prefer that I don't budge. Besides, you don't seem to be taking anything I'm saying very seriously."

Declan reached across the desk for the paper. He read the article and looked at the picture of the full moon.

"The Legend of the Blue Moon," he said. "I've never heard of it. Two full moons in one month? Must be unusual. I admit it's rather fascinating. This is quite a legend too. If the two people have chosen to be together and see the blue moon, they'll fall in love. The confirmed bachelors of the world would be shutting the door and drawing the drapes."

"You must not have a romantic bone in your body," Joy said. "Besides, it's only make-believe, the legend part, a fun, whimsical fairy tale. The appearance of the blue moon is real, though. I checked, and it's due to show itself on Saturday night."

"No joke?" Declan looked at the paper again, then back at Joy. "What if you're with some guy at the time? You know, you're out on a date and there's the blue moon. You could find yourself agreeing to marry the jerk before you know what hit you."

"Declan, don't be silly. The legend is the product of someone's imagination."

He leaned toward her. "How do you know that? You are looking, my dear, at the result of four-leaf clovers."

"I beg your pardon?"

"My folks used to live outside of LA. They're retired and living in Florida now. Anyway, they'd been married for six years, and there wasn't a baby, for no clear medical reason. One day my mom was really upset about it, so my dad took her on a picnic to cheer her up."

"That was nice of him."

"He's a great guy. Well, they found this secluded spot, and lo and behold, there was a whole field of four-leaf clovers."

"That's rather odd, isn't it?"

"It certainly is. My mom and dad had their picnic, then, well, one thing led to another, and . . . bingo . . . nine months later, there I was. Wonderful, cute-as-a-button, screaming-my-lungs-out me."

"Really? Your parents believe it was because of the four-leaf clovers?"

"You bet. On the day I was born my dad gave my mom a little china box with some of the four-leaf clovers from that field pressed under glass on the lid."

"Oh, that is so romantic. Did they have more children?"

Declan frowned. "No. Once I started moving around and destroying things, my dad said he wouldn't go back to that clover field if he was threatened with a shotgun. I was a busy, innovative little kid."

Joy laughed in delight. "What a lovely, romantic story."

"So, you see, you have to pay attention to this stuff, Joy," he said, waving the paper in the air. "Who are we to say that some of this isn't true? My parents honestly believe that if it weren't for those four-leaf clovers, I wouldn't be here. Maybe they're wrong, but who knows? This blue moon scenario is risky business."

"You're serious, aren't you?"

"Damn right, I am."

"You're a walking contradiction, Declan Harris. I keep getting the feeling that you're laughing at my remedies for stress reduction, not taking seriously what I'm saying as a trained professional. Then you turn right around and state that you believe in legends and superstitions."

"Be fair, Dr. Barlow. I'm going to put an end to my stress by watching a bunch of fish swimming around with their mouths open? I suppose exercise has something going for it because of the peptides, but fish?" He shook his head.

"You're the one not being fair, Declan," Joy said, her voice rising. "I worked and studied very hard for my degree. What I'm telling you is based on sound, scientific fact. You've only begun your stress-management program. You have to realize you can't be all and everything at your place of business. You must learn to delegate, give assignments, then trust the people to carry them out. Knowing how to relax is an art. Some people who are prone to stress work so hard at trying to relax during their leisure time, they actually create more tension within themselves."

"Look, I—"

"I'm speaking. I have tapes I can lend you that have proved to be helpful to some patients. The tape takes you on a trip of guided imagery to a quiet beach where the surf is gently lapping in a steady rhythm and—"

"Who's with me?" Declan asked, grinning and wiggling his brows.

Joy narrowed her eyes. "Forget it, just forget it. Talking to you is like trying to communicate with a wall. You are being very difficult, Mr. Harris."

"Hey, take it easy. Joy, I think we should cater to our stress a bit. We both deserve a pleasant, relaxing evening. Would you have dinner with me? Eight o'clock? Or we could exercise together, jog a few miles, get the old peptides chugging."

"No! My legs will fall off if I don't give them time to recuperate."

Declan got to his feet. "Dinner it is, then." He handed her the article about the blue moon. "You shouldn't be so narrow-minded about legends, Joy, because I'm telling you, some of this stuff is true. Oh, here's my notebook. See you later." He leaned over and gave her a searing, toe-curling kiss. "I don't have time to talk stress remedies anymore right now. I have a blueprint to check. Bye." He strode across the room and left.

"But . . ." Joy stared at the empty doorway, then looked at the picture of the full moon. "Declan Harris is really driving me crazy."

Four

Just before six o'clock Declan turned the key in the lock and entered his apartment.

"My God," he said, his eyes widening in horror as his gaze swept over the living room.

The room appeared as though a raging hurricane had torn through it, leaving nothing untouched in its path of destruction. Papers were strewn on the floor, having been pulled from the drawers of the rolltop desk. Furniture cushions were flung helter-skelter, as well as cassette tapes and videotapes. The bookcase had been swept clean, the books lying in a sickening heap on the floor.

The room had been thoroughly trashed.

"Damn," Declan muttered as a burning sensation

attacked his stomach. He strode to the telephone and yanked the receiver off the hook. His head was throbbing with such sudden, excruciating pain, his vision was blurred as he punched the numbers nine-one-one.

Just over ten minutes later Declan pushed himself away from the corridor wall as two uniformed police officers stepped out of the elevator.

"Mr. Harris?" one said as they approached him.

"Yeah. The living room is trashed, the other rooms weren't touched. As far as I can tell, nothing is missing. I used the phone to call you guys, but kept my hands off everything else. I sure as hell don't know how they got in there. The lock isn't jimmied, my key worked fine. And I can't figure out why nothing was stolen. I have some expensive stereo and video equipment in there. Hell, I don't know. I'm so ticked off I could . . ." He shook his head. "Forget it."

"Take it easy, sir," the first officer said, then turned to the other policeman. "Chuck, why don't you go down and talk to the security guard in the lobby? Ask him—" He glanced up. "Oh, man, Lieutenant Santini just got off the elevator. Why would a lieutenant of detectives respond to a call like this one? Look sharp, Chuck," he added as the tall, dark, well-built man approached. "Santini is one good, tough cop."

"Can't stay out of trouble, huh, Declan?" Vince said when he reached them.

Declan shook his hand. "It's good to see you, Vince. I knew you were back from your eighteen months in Italy on the exchange-a-cop program. Did you get my messages about getting together? I've missed our racquetball games."

"I did get the messages, but I haven't had a spare second since I stepped off the plane. I heard your call come in and decided to swing by."

Declan frowned. "My living room is blitzed."

Vince nodded. "We'll check it out."

"I was just heading for the lobby to talk with the security guard," Chuck said.

"Don't spend a lot of time doing it," Vince said. "I just walked right past him, and he never noticed. He's got his nose buried in a book. I want the lab boys over here for fingerprints."

"For this?" the other officer said. "They didn't even take anything."

"Do it."

"Oh, yes sir, Lieutenant."

"Declan," Vince said, "I'm going to take a quick look inside, then I'll buy you a cup of coffee in the café downstairs."

"Fine," Declan said glumly. "Do you have any idea what something like this can do to a man's stress level?"

• • •

Seated in a booth with Vince in the small restaurant in the lobby, Declan realized that his stomach was burning like hot lava, and he ordered cherry pie along with coffee. Vince settled for a cup of coffee. Their orders were soon placed in front of them by a cheerful waitress.

"Damn," Declan said, poking at the pie with his fork. "Why my apartment? Hell, why me?"

"That, chum, is my question."

"What do you mean?" Declan asked.

"Mildred Fairchild."

"The doctors said she was fine. It's been two years, Vince. Do you think she did this?"

"I don't know. I just don't like the timing of it, that's all. The fact that nothing was stolen doesn't sit well with me, either." He paused. "Why don't you take some aspirin for that headache you obviously have? You keep rubbing your forehead, but aspirin will do a better job."

"I gave my aspirin to Joy."

"Joy. Nice. Does she bring you the essence of her name?"

"Oh, hell, a poetic cop. You're going to push my stress level right over the edge. Bill Cooper has diagnosed me as being totally stressed out. Dr. Joy Barlow is a stress-management specialist, a psychologist. If you laugh, I'm going to punch you in the mouth."

Vince suppressed a smile. "I think it's very trendy

of you to be stressed out, Declan," he said solemnly. "So, Joy's a shrink? You are coming up in the world. A gorgeous shrink?"

"Beautiful, absolutely beautiful. I'm not an official patient, though. She's just giving me some tips, although what she prescribes is nuts in itself." He paused. "Yes, Joy is really beautiful."

"Uh-oh."

"Don't get carried away. I'm not interested in a serious commitment with a woman any more than you are. There's just something about Joy that . . . Forget it."

"Uh-oh, uh-oh," Vince said, shaking his head. "Joy's got you, friend."

"Lieutenant?"

Declan and Vince looked up to see a short bald man standing by the booth.

"Yes?" Vince said.

"Pete Mallory, lab. The place is clean. No finger-prints . . . at all. Dopers didn't do this, Lieutenant. They'd have been too spaced to go over the room that carefully."

Vince nodded. "I get the picture. Any idea how he . . . or she . . . got into the apartment?"

"Yep. Or at least I think so. Mr. Harris, do you keep a spare key taped under the third shelf of the bookcase?"

"No."

"That's it, then," Pete said. "We found one there.

He got in with a duplicate key, then left it behind to rub our noses in it."

"Thanks, Pete," Vince said. "I'll be upstairs in a few minutes."

"Okay, Lieutenant," Pete said, and walked away.

"Dammit, I don't need this hassle," Declan muttered.

"Hey, look at the bright side, buddy. You've got gorgeous Joy to hold your hand through this extremely stressful time. That's not too shabby."

"Vince?"

"Hmm?"

"Go to hell."

Vince dissolved in a fit of laughter.

Joy sat at her dressing table wrapped in a thick, fluffy lavender towel and blow-dried her freshly shampooed hair. As she turned her head, she caught a glimpse of her reflection in the oval mirror and saw the deep frown on her face.

She sighed and turned off the blow-dryer. Shaking her head, she watched in the mirror as her shiny blond hair cascaded in natural waves to the middle of her back. It felt heavenly to have her hair free and loose, not held captive at the nape of her neck. She would, she decided, wear it loose when she went out with Declan tonight.

Declan. She knew she was concentrating on her hair instead of facing a very cold and very hard fact.

Declan Harris did not respect her as a psychologist. And oh, Lord, that hurt.

It was not, Joy admitted, the first time she'd run up against someone who had preconceived, less-than-flattering opinions about psychology. She met prejudiced people everywhere, even at medical conventions. She dismissed those who rejected what they didn't understand as unimportant, and went breezily on her way. The doubters, the disbelievers, simply didn't matter.

But Declan mattered.

He mattered more with every tick of the clock and beat of her heart.

He mattered in a way no man ever had before.

Joy plunked her elbows on the dressing table and rested her chin in her hands as she stared at herself in the mirror.

Why? she asked her reflection. Why, why, why?

Unless . . .

She straightened, her eyes widening.

Unless she was falling in love with Declan Harris.

Joy smacked the top of the dressing table with the palm of one hand. "Well, dandy, just super. Joy Marilee, you are a dope." Out of the millions of men in the world, was she actually falling in love with one who was interested in only half of who she was? A man who snickered and rolled his eyes at the professional part of her, then kissed the woman part of her at every opportunity? She moaned. "Oh, darn. Oh, damn."

She sighed wearily and put on lacy pink lingerie and sheer panty hose. She applied light makeup and a spray of floral cologne, then got her dress from the closet.

It was a whisper of pale pink that seemed to float over her head like a cloud, then fit her to perfection as it settled into place. The scoop neck of the camisole top was edged in lace, and the skirt was softly gathered into another vee of lace at her waist. It was a thoroughly feminine dress, elegant and sensuous.

She brushed her hair once more, transferred the necessities to a small clutch purse that matched her high-heeled evening sandals, and nodded in approval at her reflection in the full-length mirror that hung inside her closet door.

Very nice, she decided, and certainly a change from the Joy Barlow Declan had seen thus far. He'd only seen her as a professional woman, a psychologist. And considering his kisses, his smoldering gazes, he liked what he saw.

She couldn't wait to test his reaction to this Joy Barlow!

When Declan knocked on her door, Joy paused for a moment to calm her racing heart, then opened the door. Seeing him standing on the threshold, she sighed with delight. Declan was there. In a black suit, white shirt, and black-and-pink paisley tie, gorgeous, magnificent, wonderful Declan was there.

"Hello," she murmured as she stepped back. "Come in."

Declan opened his mouth to speak, then realized nothing was going to come out and snapped it closed again. He stepped into the room, his gaze sweeping over Joy as she shut the door and turned to face him.

Never, he thought, had he seen such an exquisitely beautiful woman. Joy's hair was more sensational than he'd imagined in his wildest fantasies. And oh, Lord, that dress. The way it clung in places and swirled in others was causing his blood to heat and pound in his veins.

There was no hint of the good doctor standing before him at that moment. This was Joy, pure woman. And if he didn't take a breath in the next three seconds, he was going to pass out right at her feet.

"You," he started, trying unobtrusively to gulp air into his lungs, "are the loveliest woman I have ever seen. Your hair is . . . Oh, hell, I'm acting like a gawking adolescent, and anything I say is going to sound pretty damn corny."

"It won't sound corny," she said softly, "if you mean it."

"I mean it," he said, his voice husky. "You're beautiful, Joy Barlow."

"Thank you, Declan Harris." She walked slowly toward him. "You look marvelous too. You're an extremely handsome man."

"Thanks. Joy, I'm going to kiss you now. I really need to do that. I mean, talking to you is nice, but . . . we'll talk later. I'm kissing you now."

"You are?" she said, smiling. "As far as I can tell, you're still talking."

Declan lifted his hands, surprised to see that they were trembling, and wove his fingers through Joy's hair. A groan of ecstasy escaped from his throat. He held her head steady as he looked deeply into her eyes, then lowered his lips to hers.

She was beautiful, Joy thought dreamily. Declan was beautiful. This kiss was beautiful. And it was so right. They were just a woman and a man, not a doctor and a doubter.

She circled Declan's neck with her arms, parted her lips to receive his questing tongue, and returned the kiss with all of her passion.

This was Joy, Declan thought. The woman. His. He wanted her. Nothing was going to shatter the magic of this night. He wasn't going to think, he'd only feel and savor all that Joy the woman was. Dr. Barlow wasn't joining them. They were man and woman, nothing more. And, thank the Lord above, nothing less.

Declan raised his head and drew a ragged breath. "I made reservations for dinner," he said. "We'd better go."

"Yes, all right." Joy slowly stepped back and instantly missed Declan's heat. "I'll get my purse."

"Joy?" he said as she started to turn away.

She stopped and looked at him. "Yes?"

"Tonight could we forget how we met? What I mean is, we're a woman and a man. Let's leave the doctor, the stressed-out executive, all of that, here."

"Those things are a part of our lives, Declan."

"Not tonight."

A few stolen hours, she thought. No problems, no doubts or fears, no confusion. Just Declan. "I think that sounds lovely."

He nodded. "Good. Very good."

And probably foolish, Joy thought, as she picked up her purse, but she didn't care. Not tonight.

The moment Joy and Declan stepped out into the summer evening, their heads snapped up and their gazes swept the heavens. A heavy cloud cover revealed only a blanket of darkness. They looked at each other and burst into laughter.

"You were looking for the blue moon," Declan said, grinning. "And it's not even due yet."

"Guilty. So were you. I know the astronomers can predict the exact night it will appear, but it's so exciting that I don't want to run any risk of not seeing it."

Declan opened the passenger door of his steel-gray BMW. "And how do you feel about the legend connected to the appearance of the blue moon?"

"Oh. Well, it's . . ." She shrugged as she got into the car, then glanced up at Declan. "It's whimsical and fun, a lovely, romantic fairy tale."

"I see," he said, and shut the door with a sharp snap.

"For pete's sake," Joy muttered as he walked around to the driver's side of the car, "it certainly isn't true. Legends, superstitions, all that stuff, are only make-believe."

Declan slid behind the wheel, inserted the key in the ignition, then hesitated. He shifted in the seat and spread one arm along the top of it, gently tangling his fingers in Joy's shimmering hair.

"Joy, can't you believe in anything that isn't scientifically documented in a textbook?"

She raised one eyebrow and her chin at the same time. "Declan, can't you believe in anything that *is* scientifically documented in a textbook?"

He laughed. "Touché. The subjects of the blue moon and psychology are closed for tonight."

"So be it. However, further peeks at the sky for any sign of the blue moon are allowed."

"Yes, ma'am. Got it."

Their mingled laughter filled the car with its joyous resonance. As Declan headed for the restaurant, the lighthearted mood prevailed, and they chatted comfortably.

Yet beneath the banter and laughter a current of sensuality wove back and forth between them, spinning around them like invisible threads, binding them together. Their eyes met often, and during those fleeting collisions of green eyes and brown eyes, sentences were half-finished and thoughts forgotten as hearts skipped a beat.

The sexual tension was there, growing in intensity, swirling a demanding heat within them, which they privately acknowledged but didn't reveal to each other.

A shiver coursed through Joy.

A trickle of sweat ran down Declan's back.

"I'm sorry, sir," the young man outside the restaurant said to Declan. "I can't park your car for you. A water main broke this morning under the parking lot, and the city workers came out and tore up the whole thing. The restaurant is fine, no damage, if you'd still like to have dinner. I'll have to ask you to park on the main street, or a side street, though."

"Joy?" Declan said, looking over at her.

"That's fine, Declan. It's a lovely night, and I certainly don't mind walking. I won't even mention that walking is excellent exercise."

He chuckled. "Big of you." He looked back at the uniformed young man. "Okay, I'll find a place to park, and we'll wander back here."

"Yes, sir."

The first available parking space that Declan could find was two blocks away on a dark side street edged in trees with low-hanging branches.

"Creepy," Joy said, as they walked back to the restaurant. "There aren't even any lights on in the houses. These trees make it seem like a cave."

"There are bright lights and good food just around the corner, my sweet."

"Lead on, Mr. Harris. I'm starving."

The restaurant was known for its excellent cuisine and intimate atmosphere. Candles flickered in the centers of the linen-covered tables; the waiters wore tuxedos and spoke in hushed voices. The tables had been carefully arranged so that the patrons could forget anyone else was there, beyond the light of their candles.

Declan selected and approved a fine wine, then after they'd ordered he asked Joy about her childhood. She explained that her mother had died when she was twelve, and a soft smile touched her lips when she spoke of her father.

It was normal getting-to-know-more-about-you conversation. But still there, pulling, teasing, taunting, was the heightened awareness, the man sensing every nuance of the woman, the woman missing no detail of the man.

"When did you meet Jeff Cooper?" Joy asked at one point. She hoped Declan missed the breathless quality of her voice.

"We went to high school together. I was two years older than he was. I knew even then, had known since I was just a kid, that I wanted to be an architect. Jeff only knew he *didn't* want to be a doctor like his father."

"Bill always hoped that Jeff would become a doctor."

"I know. Anyway, Jeff finally threw up his hands and said he might as well draw something too, since that was what I did with my free time. He was instantly hooked. And talented? Lord, he had a natural ability that had somehow gone unnoticed when he was younger. We started dreaming about our future, about Harris and Cooper, Architects, and how it would be the best of its kind. Jeff said my name should come first because I was older. I went to college, he followed two years later, and finally we made it. We nearly starved at first, but . . . I miss Jeff. He was a helluva man and a good friend, and one of the most gifted architects in the business."

"Bill still misses him terribly too. I guess he always will. My father said that you pulled Bill out of a severe depression by creating the industrial physician position for him, that you literally saved his life."

"Bill was caught in his private hell of misery. I gave him a way out of it, that's all. Jeff's death was very hard for all of us to accept because he wasn't a victim of another driver, he was a victim of himself. He became consumed by the excitement of life in the fast lane, and it eventually killed him. It was all such a terrible waste, just never should have happened. I only wish I had—" He stopped speaking abruptly.

"You had what, Declan? Somehow convinced Jeff to change? That's it, isn't it? You said you're working so hard because you *owe* it to Jeff to maintain

Harris and Cooper's reputation of excellence. That's your *debt* to Jeff. Why?"

A pulse beat visibly in Declan's temple as he leaned toward her. "I was Jeff's best friend, and his business partner. I saw what was happening to him and told myself I should sit him down and have a long talk with him. But I always put it off, saying I'd do it later, when I had more time. Then—then there wasn't any more time because Jeff was dead."

"Oh, Declan," Joy said softly. She covered one of his hands with hers. "Jeff was a grown man who was responsible for his own actions. He might have listened to your advice, but I seriously doubt it. Unless he recognized his own mistakes, your words would have fallen on deaf ears. You don't owe a debt to Jeff, you really don't."

Declan met Joy's gaze, then looked at her hand covering his. He turned his over and wound his long fingers around her slender ones, his thumb stroking the side of her hand.

"I'll think about what you said," he murmured in a rough voice. "Thank you, Joy."

"You're welcome. I looked at your notebook, Declan. How hard you work for so many hours each day is there in black and white. Just like Jeff, you're responsible for your own actions. What you're doing to yourself is wrong."

He looked at her again, nodded slowly, then leaned back, his gaze locked with hers. The emotionally charged atmosphere was intruded upon by the arrival of the waiter with their dinner.

They ate and talked, and as the waiter cleared away their plates, Joy realized that if her dinner had been delicious, she certainly wasn't able to testify to the fact. She hardly remembered eating, let alone tasting anything. She saw only Declan, the candlelight accentuating the lean sharp lines of his handsome face. The night held a special magic. The night was theirs.

Neither of them wanted dessert and settled on coffee accompanied by snifters of mellow brandy.

Declan drank in the sight of Joy's delicate features as the candlelight flickered over her. Her shimmering golden hair beckoned to him to sink his hands into its lush tresses. He shifted in his chair as heat pounded through him and a knot of desire tightened deep within him.

How did a man know, he asked himself for perhaps the hundredth time since meeting Joy, if he was falling in love? Was the possessiveness he was feeling toward Joy important, shouting a message he was missing? Was the ache, the burning need he felt for her, more significant than he knew? Was the way she filled his thoughts during the days, and his dreams at night, a signal he wasn't catching due to his lack of understanding of love?

Dammit, he fumed, he was an intelligent man. Why couldn't he figure this out, unravel the tangle in his mind? Why didn't he know if he was in love with Joy Barlow?

"Declan," she said, "is something wrong with your coffee? You're certainly glaring at the cup."

"What? Oh, no, it's great coffee. I was just thinking about something else. Are you about ready to make that trek back to the car?"

"If I can move," she said, smiling. "I ate so much." Of whatever it had been. "Yes, I'm ready to go." The sooner the better, she thought. Every time she looked at Declan she felt as though she were melting like ice cream on a hot day. She needed to leave the romantic atmosphere of the restaurant and take a deep breath of clear night air. "That walk is just the ticket."

Declan nodded and signaled to the waiter for the bill.

A short time later they were strolling leisurely along the brightly lit street, then turned the corner to encounter once again the dark tunnel of the next block.

"It's still creepy," Joy said.

Declan circled her shoulders with his arm and pulled her close. "I'll protect you from ghosts and goblins and things that go bump in the night."

"That's comforting," she said, laughing softly.

They walked on, and the darkness seemed to close behind them like a heavy door.

Suddenly Declan stiffened as a tall, shadowy figure moved out of the bushes twenty feet ahead of them.

"Holy . . ." he started.

"What's wrong?" Joy asked. "I—"

Before she could say more, Declan wrapped his arms around her and flung them both face down onto the grass next to the sidewalk. Declan's weight pinned her to the ground.

A scream caught in Joy's throat as she froze in fear.

Declan lifted his head and peered into the darkness.

"Here, Tippy, here boy," a deep voice called in the distance. "There you are, you naughty dog. Get back in the house."

Declan's head dropped to Joy's shoulder as he closed his eyes in relief. He moved off Joy and stretched out next to her, turning her to face him.

"Care to explain?" she asked politely.

"I'm sorry. Are you all right? Did I hurt you? I'm really edgy, I guess. I found someone had broken into my apartment when I got home tonight. When I saw that guy come out of the bushes, I thought . . . Oh, Lord, I'm a jerk."

"No, you're not," Joy said. "And, no, I'm not hurt. I was surprised, that's all. One minute we were walking along and the next . . ."

"I know, I know. I'm really sorry." He chuckled. "Well, not completely, because lying here with you on this sweet-smelling grass is not cause for complaint." He lowered his lips to hers. "Not at all."

The kiss began softly, then intensified as tongues met in the brandy-flavored darkness of Joy's mouth. Joy clung to the front of Declan's jacket as he held her to him, one hand stroking across her back. The grass was a plush, fragrant bed, the darkness a cocoon of privacy.

They were in a world of their own that contained only the two of them.

And heat. And an ever-growing desire within them. An aching need like none either of them had ever known.

Declan tore his lips from hers. "Joy," he said hoarsely, "this isn't the place. Or the time. Or . . . oh, hell. I want you so much, so damn much."

"I want you too, Declan," she whispered, hardly able to breathe.

He gazed into her eyes for a long moment. "Joy, let's go home."

Five

"And that's the whole story," Declan said as they entered Joy's apartment. "The doctors say that Mildred Fairchild is perfectly sane. Vince, obviously, has his doubts. He's determined to talk to her. I'm afraid he'll do it even if he doesn't get clearance. Vince is a bit of a maverick cop. He gets sick to death of the politics and red tape of the department."

"Declan, do you think Mildred Fairchild is the one who trashed your apartment?"

He placed his hands on her shoulders. "I don't know." He paused. "I apologize again for overreacting when I saw that man on the street. Are you positive I didn't hurt you?" He pulled her to him, holding her tightly.

"I'm fine," she said, nestling her head on his chest. She inhaled his aroma, felt his strength and heat, and sighed in pleasure. "Just fine. I look like a wreck at the moment, but I'm no worse for wear."

Declan moved her away just enough to be able to look down at her. She lifted her head and met his warm gaze.

"You look beautiful," he said, lowering his head toward hers. "You always look beautiful."

His mouth came down hard on hers in a kiss that was urgent and frenzied, speaking of hours spent holding passion at bay. Passion that now demanded to be set free.

His arousal was instantaneous, pressing against her soft body as his tongue plummeted deep into her mouth. His hands tangled in her luxuriant hair, then roamed over her back, down to the slope of her buttocks. He spread his legs and fit her to the cradle of his hips. A groan rumbled deep in his chest.

Joy wrapped her arms around Declan's back, feeling his muscles bunch and move, even through the layers of clothes. She returned the hungry demands of his lips and tongue, holding nothing back, giving as she received.

Her breasts were crushed to the hard wall of his chest, and she savored the sweet pain. His arousal was strong and full against her, and her heart sang with the wondrous knowledge that he wanted her as much as she did him.

Because, oh, yes, she wanted to make love with Declan Harris. Now.

There were no thoughts beyond her burning need for this man. Confusion, doubts, questions, would not be allowed to intrude upon their ecstasy. This night was theirs.

Declan lifted his head a fraction of an inch. "Joy?"

"Yes," she whispered.

That "yes" would change her life. She knew without a single doubt that making love with Declan would mean she would never be the same again. The future was shrouded in a hazy mist, nothing clearly visible. There was only this night, this moment, in crystal clarity. There was only Declan.

"Yes," she repeated softly.

Arms around each other, their bodies pressed close, they crossed the living room and entered the dark bedroom. Joy stepped away to snap on a small lamp on the nightstand, its light casting a rosy glow over the room. Then she turned to face Declan.

He walked slowly toward her, absently noticing that the room was feminine and pretty, a vibrant spread of multicolored wildflowers on the double bed.

The decor was forgotten when he stopped in front of Joy and saw in her eyes the smoky hue of desire he knew was reflected in his own. Their want was equal, their desire at the same fever pitch. What was given would be received; what received, given, in mutual sharing.

He knew that this joining, this intimate act, would be like nothing he'd experienced before.

Because this was Joy.

While their gazes still held, Joy reached behind her and undid the zipper of the filmy dress. She brushed the straps of the camisole top down her arms, and the dress floated to the floor.

Declan's gaze swept over Joy's scantily clad figure and his manhood surged with desire. He shrugged out of his jacket, pulled his tie free, and flung them onto a nearby chair.

Without once looking away from each other, they removed the remainder of their clothes and stood before each other naked.

"Joy," Declan murmured. He lifted a shaking hand and placed it gently on her cheek. "You're exquisite."

She turned her head to kiss his palm, then her gaze slid slowly over him, over every magnificent inch of him.

His body was lean and hard and tanned. Dark hair curled enticingly on his broad chest, glistening with moisture. He was fully aroused, his manhood a bold announcement of his masculinity and his want of her.

This was man, Joy thought, her man. He was tall and powerful, but she knew he would temper his strength with gentleness when he brought to her all that he was.

He was Declan, and the sheer beauty of him caused quick tears to mist her eyes, and a smile to touch her lips.

"You're exquisite too, Declan," she whispered, meeting his gaze again.

He closed the short distance separating them and drew her into his arms, his mouth seeking hers. Their lips met, their tongues met, their bodies met. Heat spread from one into the other as their heartbeats raced and breathing quickened.

There were no barriers between them, neither clothes, nor doubts. They were free to give way to the desire that consumed them, holding nothing back.

When Declan reluctantly lifted his head, he looked deep into Joy's eyes for a long moment, then stepped over to the bed and swept the blankets back.

He turned again and lifted her into his arms, placing her in the center of the cool white sheets. His gaze swept over her as he remained standing by the bed, memorizing the lush bounty of her breasts, every inch of her soft curves and long legs, her hair spread out on the pillow like a golden aureole. Her skin was satiny and gleaming with a dewy, peachy hue.

A strange ache tightened his throat, and he swallowed heavily before stretching out next to her. He splayed one hand flat on her stomach as he leaned over her.

"I want you so much," she said, her voice hushed. "So very much, Declan."

The lump in his throat grew, and he kissed her, rather than attempting to speak. His hand moved up from her stomach to cup one breast, his thumb stroking the nipple to a taut button. His tongue drew lazy circles around hers, then he moved his lips to where his hand had been, and sucked the sweet flesh of her breast. His manhood surged hard against her thigh as his hand roamed over her stomach once again, then lower.

A soft sigh of pleasure escaped Joy's lips as she wove her fingers through the thick night darkness of Declan's hair, urging his mouth more firmly onto her breast. Heat and tingling desire swirled within her, and her eyes drifted closed as she savored it all.

Declan's hand moved lower yet to the heated center of her. His fingers were instruments of sweet torture, tantalizing, teasing, creating a pulsing rhythm deep within her that matched the pull of his mouth on her breast.

"Oh, Declan," she whispered. "Please. I need you. I want you."

He left her breast to seek the other one. "Soon," he said, his voice harsh with passion. "Soon, Joy."

He drew her other breast deep into his mouth, laving the nipple with his tongue, as his fingers continued to stroke her moist heat. She tossed her head restlessly on the pillow as tension grew within her, tightening, demanding release.

Declan's muscles quivered from forced restraint as he waited. He had to know that Joy was ready for him.

This had to be perfect for her, he thought in a passion-laden haze. Her pleasure must be assured before he'd take his own. He had to wait, be certain that he wouldn't hurt her. He ached to bury himself deep, so deep, within her, sheath himself in the silken heat that his fingers now stroked. No, he had to wait . . . wait. . . .

Joy was aware of the trembling of Declan's taut, muscled body, and even through the fiery desire that seemed to be consuming her entire being, she knew he was holding back, controlling himself so she would have her pleasure first.

Never before had she felt so special, so cherished. But she wanted Declan . . . now. Needed him now. She couldn't bear to wait another heartbeat to become one with him, to have his body meshed with hers.

She slid her fingers through the moist curls on his chest, then lower. His stomach muscles jerked beneath her feathery touch. He left her breast to claim her mouth in a searing kiss, his tongue delving deep into her to find her tongue. Her hand slipped lower. A groan rumbled in Declan's chest.

She found him, all that he was, all he would bring to her.

Declan lost control.

"Joy," he moaned.

She gazed up at him. "Now," she whispered.

He hesitated no longer.

He moved over her and into her, and they were one.

"Oh, yes, yes," Joy said, entwining her arms around him.

He began to move, slowly at first, then quickening the tempo. Joy matched him eagerly, and the rhythm increased to a thundering cadence.

Tension built in dark, secret places, struggling to break free. The promise of ecstasy teased and tantalized them, and Declan drove deeper within Joy as she wrapped her legs around his powerful thighs and urged him on. She lifted her hips and strained against him as she drew closer and closer . . .

"Declan!"

"Oh, yes. That's it, Joy. Now!"

She clung to him as waves of exquisite sensations crashed over her, her body tightening around him as she was carried up and over the brink of reality.

He plunged one last time, then shuddered, his life's force spilling into her as he found his own release. A groan that was pure male pleasure escaped from his lips, then he collapsed against her, sated, his strength gone. He buried his face in the fragrant cloud of her hair, his breathing still rough.

Slowly, very slowly, they drifted back from where they had gone together. Breathing quieted, hearts resumed beating in normal tempos, bodies cooled.

But neither moved nor spoke.

Neither wished to break the magical spell that still encased them in a private cocoon that nothing from the outside world could enter.

Finally Declan stirred and shifted his weight to his forearms, his gaze tracing Joy's features. The flush of passion was still on her cheeks, and her lips were curved in a sweet smile.

"You were wonderful," he said quietly.

"We were wonderful together. I've never experienced anything so glorious, Declan."

"I feel the same way, Joy. It . . . we were incredible." He brushed his lips over hers. "I'd better move off you. I must be smashing you."

"No, you're not." She drew her fingers through his hair. "I adore your hair."

He chuckled. "Really? I'm rather crazy about your hair. It's beautiful. *You're* beautiful. I tried to imagine how long your hair was, what it would look like loose. When I saw you standing there tonight in that dress, your hair like a golden waterfall, I . . . well, you really bowled me over." He smiled. "It's not very macho of me to admit that, is it?" The smile faded. "But it's true, Joy. Confusing as hell, but true."

"*Shh,*" she said, placing a finger against his lips. "Don't talk about anything confusing or disturbing. There's nothing beyond the private world we've created right here." She traced the outline of his lips with the tip of her finger.

"I thought you psychologist types insisted that . . . Joy, you're driving me crazy doing what you're doing . . . that people face whatever's bothering them."

She ran her finger across each of his dark eyebrows, down his straight nose, then retraced the shape of his lips.

"I'm not speaking as a psychologist, but as a woman," she said.

His tongue darted out to flick against her busy finger. "Oh, well, that's fine then. I seem to naturally zero in on the woman that's you. Joy, the woman, is the one who is turning me inside out." His manhood stirred within her as she continued her teasing foray across his lips. "And Joy the woman had better be aware of what she's doing to me."

"Oh, yes, I can feel what's happening to you inside me, Declan. We're two individual people, but together, like this, we're one, and it's only as one that we can go to that glorious place."

Declan lowered his head and spoke with his mouth against hers. "Then fly with me, Joy. Fly up, and over, and away."

They did. As one they soared, sharing the passion

rocketing through them. They were lifted up and away to the rapturous place they sought, their bodies joined in the wild, earthy dance of love.

Only a heartbeat apart, they burst free and, calling each other's name, were flung into ecstasy.

They lingered there, savoring the sensations still drifting through them, clinging to each other.

Slowly they floated back to reality.

"Oh, my," Joy whispered.

"No joke," Declan said. "Incredible."

He reached out to snap off the light, then nestled her close to his side, his fingers sifting through her silken hair. He kissed her gently on the forehead, then pulled the blankets over their cooling bodies.

"Sleepy?" he asked.

"Very, and very contented."

"I don't think I could move if someone yelled, 'Fire.' "

"Good. Don't move." She yawned. "Good night, Declan."

"Night," he said, still drawing his fingers through her hair.

Good night? he thought. It had been much better than good. It was a night he wouldn't soon forget, maybe never forget. A truly fantastic night. The lovemaking he'd shared with Joy had been so much more than physical pleasure. He'd felt . . . whole, filled to overflowing with something he couldn't put a name to.

He shifted slightly into a more comfortable position, then blanked his mind and drifted off to sleep with Joy tucked safely by his side.

Joy pulled herself from the disturbing dream, and a shiver of relief swept through her as she realized she was now awake and the nightmare was over.

Her hand was resting on Declan's chest, and she left it there, feeling the steady, slow rhythm of his breathing. She was stretched along the side of his muscled body, his natural warmth causing curls of desire to tingle within her.

How magnificent their lovemaking had been, she mused. Indescribably exquisite in its splendor, it had also been wonderfully honest as they both gave and received, holding nothing back.

She sighed. She wished she hadn't had that dream. It had been so vivid, so real. An evil man had been waiting for her in the shadows of a dark street, ready to attack her. She'd run away in terror, searching for Declan and the safe haven of his arms. Her hair had been loose, whipping around her face, and she'd been wearing the camisole dress.

Declan had appeared, urgently beckoning to her, telling her to hurry. But as she ran, she changed, suddenly finding herself in a dark, tailored suit, her hair twisted into a bun at the back of her head.

Declan had frowned as she approached him, then he'd stepped back and said the hateful words. He did not have room in his life for Dr. Joy Barlow, the psychologist. Only Joy the woman was welcome there. She'd pleaded with him to see that she was both Joys, she was a combination of the two, needing each to complete the picture of who she really was.

But Declan had shaken his head and moved farther back, closing an enormous door that had suddenly appeared. Joy had screamed in distress before turning and flattening herself against the door, watching in horror as the faceless man came toward her in slow motion.

Joy raised up on one arm and gazed down at Declan sleeping so close to her. Oh, Declan, she thought. Her feelings for him were growing. The emotions were still a maze of confusion, but were insisting she face them.

And earlier, in that bed, Declan had said, "I seem naturally to zero in on the woman part of you. Joy, the woman, is the one who is turning me inside out."

Tears misted her eyes as she eased back onto the pillow and stared up at the dark ceiling. Declan was still there, next to her, his warm body pressed to hers, yet she suddenly felt chilled and totally alone.

"Oh, God." She pressed trembling fingers to her lips to keep a sob from escaping.

Declan wanted only Joy the woman. He'd made love with Joy the woman, laughed, smiled, shared with that part of her. Dr. Joy Barlow had been shoved into the shadows and ignored by him, and he refused to acknowledge her presence unless forced to do so. He cared about only half of who she was.

As Joy lay in the darkness with silent tears trickling down her cheeks, she knew the sad, lonely truth.

It would never be enough.

Six

Joy walked slowly across the parking lot toward the restaurant. She was delaying meeting her father and chided herself for acting like a child caught with her hand in the cookie jar.

After all, she told herself, it wasn't printed on her forehead that she'd spent the night with Declan, made beautiful love with Declan, had experienced that morning Declan's sensuous kiss and knowing touch, which had been followed by more exquisite lovemaking. She wasn't a walking neon sign declaring all that had transpired between her and Declan Harris.

But fathers were fathers, and she now wished she hadn't agreed to meet hers for lunch. He'd called after Declan had left the apartment to keep a raquetball date with Vince, and Joy had had no plausible reason for not having lunch with him.

She sighed, opened the door to the restaurant, and a minute later sat down opposite her father at the table where he'd been waiting for her.

"Hi, Dad," she said brightly, not quite meeting his eyes. "How are you on this sunny Saturday?"

"Fine, fine, and you? You seem chipper."

"Chipper? Oh, yes, that's me. Chipper Joy. I have no reason not to be chipper so . . ." Her voiced trailed off weakly. ". . . I'm . . . chipper."

"I see," Jack said, chuckling softly.

Her eyes widened. "You do?"

"Are you ready to order?" a waitress asked, a pencil poised over a pad.

"Yes," Joy said, snatching the menu from the table. "What are you having, Dad?"

Jack chuckled again and picked up his menu. They placed their orders, and the waitress moved away.

"Well, Miss Chipper," Jack said, "what's new with Declan Harris? Since you're chipper instead of shook up, am I to assume that all is well with Declan?"

"Yes, sort of. No, not exactly," Joy said, fiddling with her napkin. She slowly met her father's gaze. "Declan is very special, Dad. He makes me feel . . .

What I mean is, I have never felt so . . . However, I . . ."

"Joy," Jack interrupted, "talk to your old dad. I can tell you're growing very fond of Declan. I think that's wonderful, but something is obviously wrong."

"Oh, Dad, I'm terribly confused. I do care for Declan, could even be falling in love with him for all I know, but unless he changes his views about my career, we're in for a rough time."

"Go on," Jack said. "I'm listening."

"I know there are some medical doctors who view psychologists' offices as handy places to send patients who have nothing physically wrong with them but who crave attention, need someone to listen to them on a one-to-one basis."

"That attitude of doctors is nothing new to you, Joy. You've run into it in the past."

"I know, and I've always ignored anyone who denigrates my profession, because I believe in what I'm doing. I've seen proof that I can help those who come to me. But this is Declan, and it's very hard to deal with the fact that he rolls his eyes and shakes his head at the notion that seeing a psychologist can give more to a person than something to talk about at a party. Declan is interested only in Joy the woman. Dr. Joy Barlow be damned."

Jack nodded, but kept silent as the waitress set their lunches in front of them. Joy poked at her chef's salad while Jack took a bite of his steak sandwich.

"Declan's attitude hurts a lot," Jack said finally. "Doesn't it?"

"Yes," she said, meeting her father's gaze. "Yes, it hurts very much."

"Joy, you must remember that Declan is a product of whatever environment he grew up in and the social circle he moves in now. The only frame of reference he has for psychologists is probably what he's heard from other people."

Joy shook her head. "I can imagine some of the things he could have heard from all of those bored people who think being in therapy is *the* thing to do. I can spot people like that after one session, and I tell them they have no need for my help." She paused. "Oh, darn it, Dad, I can't be in a relationship with a man who is interested only in half of who I am."

"I understand that, but Declan can't be expected to change his views overnight. He needs time to take a closer look at just what this profession of yours is all about. You, young lady, are going to have to be patient. You've found a special man, and you want everything to be perfect. Life, unfortunately, doesn't always work that way."

Joy jabbed her fork into a chunk of cheese. "Well, you certainly told me, Dr. Barlow. I should quit acting like such a spoiled brat and be patient, give Declan time to learn just what it is that I do."

Jack nodded. "That about sizes it up. Eat your lunch and quit pouting. I'm playing golf with Bill Cooper this afternoon, and at the rate you're *not* eating your lunch, I'll never get there on time."

"You've spoken with Bill? Did he tell you that Mildred Fairchild, the mother of the girl who was killed with Jeff, has been released from the sanitarium?"

"No, he didn't mention it. Why?"

"I just wondered. Declan's apartment was trashed, and Vince Santini, a detective friend of Declan's, is trying to get clearance to question Mildred Fairchild."

"She threatened a great many people at the time of the accident, didn't she?"

"Yes, but the doctors have declared her to be fine now."

"They'll be protective of her, you know. She has to start a new life for herself, and her doctors won't look kindly upon a police officer who insists she be accountable for her whereabouts. I'll ask Bill this afternoon what he thinks of all this. If I ever get to the golf course. Would you please eat?"

"Yes, yes, all right, I'm eating." She shoveled in a bite of salad. "See?"

"Don't talk with your mouth full."

"Once a father, always a father."

"Who loves you very much."

"I know, Dad," she said, smiling at him warmly. "I know."

Declan and Vince left the health club and walked along the crowded sidewalk toward the restaurant they'd chosen for lunch.

"Feel better now?" Declan asked. "You won every game and nearly wiped me out in the process. That ought to have taken care of *your* stress level. Besides, Vince, it's not as though your captain didn't listen to you and take some action."

"Yeah, right," Vince said gruffly. "He called Mildred Fairchild's doctor and told him what's been going on since she got out of the sanitarium. The doc claims that Mildred is so together there would be no problem with her being asked where she was the day your apartment was broken into."

"But she's not in LA."

"Right. She was going to go visit her sister in Florida before she moved back into her house permanently. The tenants who had been renting it have left already. And no, he didn't know Mildred's sister's name. So, I'm back to square one. Is she really in Florida, or hiding out somewhere here? I intend to get some answers."

"Lord, you're a stubborn Italian."

"I sure am. How's Joy?"

"I need to talk to you about that. Let's get inside and settled at a table."

Vince nodded in agreement.

After the waitress had taken their orders, Declan let out a long breath and looked at Vince. "Okay, here it is. Get serious about what I'm saying, all right?"

"Sure, Declan. What's wrong?"

"It's Joy. I . . . Vince, if I was falling in love with her, I'd know it, wouldn't I?"

"You're asking me? I've never been in love. Maybe you just have a case of overactive lust."

"No, it's more than that because emotions are involved and . . . dammit, this is crazy. I don't want to be in love now. Not, of course, that I know if I'm falling in love. How's a guy supposed to know? And besides, Vince, Joy and I are an argument waiting to happen because of her career. Ready for this? She says watching fish swimming around in a tank is helpful in reducing stress. Fish. Can you believe that?"

"Yes, as a matter of fact, I can. A psychiatrist came to speak to the heads of departments of the police force about cop burnout, the huge divorce rate, stress, all of that. He said exactly what you're saying about the fish. We were going to buy the captain a tank with a piranha in it, but we chickened out. Your lady knows what she's talking about.

I get the feeling you're not high on her profession. What have you got against the science of psychology?"

"The fish actually . . ." Declan shook his head. "I'll be damned. I was wrong about the exercise too. It does reduce stress because it releases something into your system called peptides. Oh, hell, I don't know, Vince. It just seems like at every party I've been to in the past couple of years, people were bragging about being in therapy. Even my date was liable to say something hokey like, 'My analyst says I need to discover my true inner self.' Going to those kinds of doctors has been the trendy thing to do, and I ignored it all, didn't take any of it seriously. I figured the shrinks were making a bundle from people who were bored and had plenty of money to waste."

"Joy would be thrilled to hear you say all this," Vince said dryly.

"Well, hell, would you be impressed by someone who tells you to exercise until you're dying, then stare at some fish? So, okay, there's merit to what Joy said, I guess, but . . . I like her . . . Hell, I more than like her. Her. Joy. The woman. So what if I'm not all charged up over what she does for a living?"

"So what?" Vince leaned forward, resting his elbows on the table. "You're kidding yourself, buddy. Hey, it's fine if all you want is a quick affair with Joy. But suppose this is more, something really special? Suppose, Declan, that you really are falling in love with her? Then your 'so what' attitude won't wash. Why do you think there are so many divorced cops? Their wives just never got a grip on what that guy goes through out there. It's not her fault; it's not his. It's just the way it is. Those people, the cop and his wife, can't say 'so what' and keep it together. Joy isn't just a beautiful woman, Declan. She's a doctor in a specialized field. You'd better get a handle on that, respect it, or get out of her life right now."

Declan glared at Vince. "Since when are you such an expert on relationships with women? You're a bed-hopper, Santini. You don't commit yourself long enough for the sheets to cool."

"Damn right I don't, because I made my choice a long time ago. Be a cop, or be a husband and father. You? If you're falling in love, Declan, you'd better respect your lady . . . all of her . . . the way she is."

"You're so smug," Declan said, "I hope you fall hard and fast for some woman and have to suffer through this heaven and hell."

"Never happen."

"Oh, yeah? I do believe I said something like that on more than one occasion in the past. Then I met Joy Barlow."

"A beautiful woman, who also happens to be a . . ."

"Psychologist." Declan shook his head. "I definitely have some serious thinking to do."

"You—" Vince started, but a quiet buzzing sound interrupted him. He pressed a button on the small black box attached to his belt. "My beeper. I'll call in and be right back."

"Okay," Declan said absently. Dammit, why in the hell had Joy picked such a screwball profession? And how was he supposed to fall all over himself telling her it was the greatest thing since sliced bread? Lord, what a mess. What a crummy, rotten, lousy mess.

Vince reappeared at the table, but didn't sit down. "Forget lunch. Let's go. You're involved in this, so you might as well see it firsthand."

Declan got to his feet. "See what? Where are we going?"

"To my office. An envelope was found on my desk with my name on it, cut out of letters from a newspaper. They couldn't reach me earlier because my beeper was in the locker room while we were playing raquetball. They contacted the captain, and he had the bomb boys open it."

"Lord. And?"

"It was a note, Declan." His voice was low so that only Declan could hear him. "Like my name on the envelope it was made from cut-out letters."

"What did it say?"

"Ready? It said, 'All will pay for past sins. Yours in death, Jeff Cooper.' "

"Vince, that note is nuts. It sounds like someone

is avenging Jeff's death, but the accident was his fault. That doesn't make sense."

"A sick mind rarely does."

"Mildred Fairchild?"

Vince ran his hand over the back of his neck. "I don't know, but I'm sure as hell going to find out. Coming?"

"Damn right, I am. Joy's been seen with me now, and she could be in danger too. Nothing is going to happen to her, Vince. I swear, *nothing* is going to happen to her."

Joy straightened the waistband of her pale blue sweater over her jeans and hurried to answer the knock at her apartment door. As she opened the door, an instant smile lit up her face.

"Hello, Declan," she said. "Come in." Declan in jeans and a green knit shirt. Scrumptious. "Did you enjoy your raquetball with Vince this morning?" She closed the door and turned to face him, seeing the frown now on his face. "What's wrong?"

Without saying a word, he pulled her into his arms and kissed her.

Even as desire threatened to consume her reasoning, Joy was aware of the coiled tension in Declan's body. He was holding her so tightly she could hardly breathe, and the kiss was rough, urgent, his tongue delving deep into her mouth. She pulled herself back from the hazy mist of passion, flattened her hands on his chest, and pushed.

She gasped. "Declan."

"What?" he said, appearing momentarily confused. He shook his head. "Oh, Joy, I'm sorry." He released her, then tenderly cradled her face in his hands. "Did I hurt you?" A deep frown knitted his brows as he searched her face. "Joy?"

"No, you didn't hurt me, but something is obviously wrong. You're so tense, it's a wonder your bones aren't creaking."

"Could happen," he said, managing a smile. "I feel old enough for creaking bones at the moment. Holy smokes, I bet my stress level is at the top of the scale." He frowned again. "The truth of the matter is, I have a roaring headache. I might as well admit it, Dr. Barlow. I'm stressed out to the max."

"Well, Mr. Harris," she said, smiling warmly, "maybe you should come sit down and talk over what's bothering you."

He circled her shoulders with his arm and led her to the sofa. When they were seated close together, he looked at her.

"I realize that I disappeared on you all day," he said, "then called tonight and said I'd be right over. That wasn't exactly socially acceptable behavior, and I apologize. I've been with Vince."

"And?"

"You couldn't pay me enough to be a cop. The

stuff that goes on in the station house alone is grim. Anyway, Vince got a sort of threatening note, made from letters cut out of the newspaper."

"My Lord, just like in the movies."

"It's not exciting in real life, believe me. It's just plain creepy. The note said that all would pay for past sins and was signed in those cut-out letters with Jeff Cooper's name."

"But Jeff is . . ."

"Dead. I know, and it's really crazy because the car crash was his fault. The note made it sound as though his death is being avenged, but he caused the accident himself. I spent hours with Vince and his lab people. They're amazing. They determined what kind of paste was used, the brand of paper the note was constructed on, the fact that the letters were cut from the LA *Times*, the manufacturer of the envelope. Interesting, but worthless information, actually, because there was nothing unique about any of the supplies used. No one knows how the envelope got on Vince's desk. There are always a lot of people milling around, and it was just suddenly there."

"Fingerprints?"

"Nope, nothing. Joy, there is someone out there who isn't playing with a full deck, and I'm half out of my mind with worry that you're in danger."

"Me? I told you that I hadn't even seen Jeff for several years before he died."

"I realize that, but you *have* been seen with *me*. Until Vince can find Mildred Fairchild, talk to her, and convince himself that she's innocent, he feels everyone she originally threatened when her daughter was killed is in danger. He can't be positive that the list now includes you because you've been with me, but I, for one, am not taking any chances."

"Meaning?"

"Meaning . . . I think I should stay completely away from you to give the appearance that we went out a few times, it was no big deal, and that was that."

Joy leaned forward until her nose was nearly touching Declan's. "Isn't that a bit drastic?"

"Temptation, thy name is Joy." He gave her a fast, hard kiss on the lips.

She straightened. "Stop that. Declan, you're only guessing that I'm in danger. In fact, you don't even know for certain that Mildred Fairchild is involved in any of this. I don't like outside forces controlling my life, not at all. I don't think we should stop seeing each other because of a 'maybe.' "

"I'm not crazy about this plan, either." He got to his feet and towered over her. "But you're important to me, dammit, so quit giving me such a hard time and do this my way."

Joy stood and glared at him. "I don't—"

"Listen to me, please," he said, his voice gentling. He held her shoulders with a touch as gentle as his voice. "You can't deny that something is happening between us, Joy. Personally, I haven't figured out just what that something is, but I do know this much. I couldn't handle it if anything happened to you." He gave her a little shake. "Joy, can you deny there's something very special between us? You feel it, don't you? Don't you, Joy?"

"Yes," she whispered.

He lifted his hands to weave his fingers through her silken hair. "I'd give anything if Mildred Fairchild, or whoever it is, wasn't out there causing all this hassle. I want to concentrate on you, us, find answers to so many questions." He dipped his head and brushed his lips over hers. She shivered from the sensual impact of that fleeting caress. "I have to stay away from you for now, Joy. I need to know that you're safe. Do you understand?"

"Yes, I—I need to know that you're safe too. Oh, Declan, there are so many questions without answers, just like you said. I'm so confused, and I hate feeling this way."

"When we do have a chance to shut the door and close out all and everything beyond it, the world we create is ours. Just the two of us, Joy, together." He lowered his lips to hers. "Lord, how I want you."

His mouth melted over hers, and Joy parted her lips to welcome the sensual stroking of his tongue. Her arms floated up to entwine his neck, her fingers inching into his thick hair.

She leaned against him, pressing her breasts to

his chest. Breasts which grew heavy, aching for the soothing, yet tantalizing, feel of Declan's strong hands and the exquisite sensation of his mouth on her soft flesh.

Declan's hands slid over her hair, then down to her hips to nestle her to him, his arousal full and heavy, surging against her. He broke away only long enough to lift her onto the sofa, then followed her down, catching his weight on his forearms. His mouth captured hers again in a hungry kiss of want, and need, and desire, that consumed them like a flash fire.

Declan groaned. Joy purred. His hand slipped beneath her sweater to find one breast, his thumb stroking the nipple until it tightened and strained against the wispy lace of her bra.

"Oh, Declan, please," she whispered. "Don't make me wait. I want you so much."

He gazed into her brown eyes, seeing the desire that he knew was mirrored in his own eyes. They were one in mind, and soon they would be one in body.

"Declan?"

"Yes," he said hoarsely. "I want you. Now."

With an economy of motion he skimmed Joy's clothes from her slender body, then his own clothes followed to land in a heap on the floor. His hands cupped her breasts, then his mouth sought the bounty of one as he stretched out alongside her again, his leg pinning hers. She arched her back to offer more, to take more, wanting more.

His lips left her breast to move lower, trailing a ribbon of kisses along her dewy skin. Lower. Lower. To the heat of her, the essence of her femininity.

"Oh, Declan," she said on a near sob. "Please come to me. I want . . . I need to feel you inside of me."

He shifted upward, claiming her mouth in a hard, searing kiss.

And then he filled her, sheathing his aching manhood in the velvety heat that welcomed him, took him, received all that he was. There was no slow, tentative lovemaking, but an instant pounding, raging rhythm that Joy met and matched eagerly, holding nothing back.

They flew to the edge of the abyss, hovered there for a heartbeat, then tumbled over a breath apart, clinging to each other as shattering pleasure consumed them.

Then in stillness and sated contentment they lay meshed as one, savoring.

Time ceased to exist. They were together, and nothing else mattered.

Finally Declan lifted his head from the fragrant pillow of Joy's hair and brushed his lips over hers. He eased himself off her and out of her, aware of his reluctance to leave the welcoming haven of her body. He stayed by her side, his weight on one forearm, and smiled down at her.

"Hello," she whispered serenely.

He chuckled. "Do I say, 'Fancy meeting you here'? How about, 'What's a nice girl like you doing naked on the sofa?' *Hmm?* Answer that one."

"This nice girl is naked on the sofa because she just made exquisite love with"—The man she loved?—"a very special man."

"Ah, I see. That explains it then. What a coincidence, ma'am. I just made love with a very special woman." Was he in love with Joy? He needed to know. "Fantastic, beautiful, incredible love." He paused. "I hate to break the mood, Joy, but we have to back up and scream and holler some more about my not seeing you until Vince figures out what's going on with Mildred Fairchild."

She sighed. "I just don't like the idea that I'm forced into a situation by someone I don't even know."

"I understand that. Look, Vince is raising the roof to get action taken on this matter. That is one angry cop, let me tell you. I really don't think it's going to drag on for long. In the meantime I don't want—"

"Me in danger by being seen with you," she finished for him. "*Maybe* in danger."

The telephone rang.

"You have *not* been saved by the bell," Declan said, reaching over to the end table to grab the receiver. He handed it to Joy. "We're going to settle this."

She frowned at him, then greeted the caller.

"Joy? It's Dad. I'm sorry to bother you, honey, but I'm just so damn upset. . . ."

"Dad, what is it? What's wrong?"

"It's Butch. Joy, he's been poisoned. I'm here at the vet's, Dr. Timbers. He doesn't know if Butch is going to make it. Butch is fighting, but he's twelve years old, and . . . I love that old dog, I really do."

"So do I. I'll be right there, Dad. I want to be with you and Butch. Dear heaven, who would do such a thing to a gentle animal like Butch? Never mind. I'm on my way."

"Thanks, sweetheart."

Declan replaced the receiver, then leveled himself up to sit on the edge of the sofa. "Butch?" he asked, reaching for his clothes.

She stood up, unmindful of her nakedness.

"I'll take a quick shower and grab clean clothes."

"Wait a minute. What's going on?"

"Butch, our family dog, has been poisoned. Oh, Declan, my father sounded so distraught. I've got to get to the vet's."

"I'll drive you."

"Yes, all right. Who would do such a horrible thing? Butch never hurt anyone." She started toward the bedroom. "What kind of person would intentionally try to kill a sweet, loving animal like Butch?"

"Joy," Declan said quietly.

She stopped and turned halfway to face him. "Yes?"

"The same kind of person who trashes apartments and pastes threatening notes together."

"You think this is connected to . . ." Her eyes widened. "Why? Because I know you, my father is related to me, and Butch is his dog? Declan, that's insane."

"Maybe I'm way off base on this, but I'm not taking any chances. You go get dressed, and I'll try to locate Vince by phone. What's the name of the vet we're going to?"

"Dr. Timbers on Eighth Street. Oh, God, Declan, this is frightening."

"I know." He reached for the telephone. "Believe me, Joy, I know."

Seven

Joy rushed through the door of the veterinarian's office with Declan right behind her. Jack was instantly on his feet, and Joy hugged him tightly.

"How's Butch?" she asked, searching her father's face for an answer.

"I don't know. I shouldn't have called you, Joy. I'm acting like a foolish old dotard. I just suddenly couldn't face sitting here alone, waiting, wondering if Butch was going to . . ." Emotion choked off his words. "I'm really very sorry."

"When I was about ten," Declan said quietly, "my mom, dad, and I spent an entire night out in the rain searching for our dog, Pepper. We staggered in at dawn, wet and exhausted . . . but we hadn't found

Pepper. That hound crawled out from under my bed and greeted us with a wagging tail and what I swear was a smile. My dad wouldn't speak to Pepper for a week. Believe me, sir, I understand what it's like to love a dog. He's a member of the family, no doubt about it. By the way, I'm Declan Harris."

Joy stared at Declan, tears misting her eyes. He had shared the tale about Pepper to ease her father's embarrassment over his emotional reaction to Butch's poisoning.

There were such depths of caring within Declan, she mused. He continually surprised her by revealing another dimension of himself, a side of him she hadn't seen before. And each new layer that she discovered caused her feelings for him to grow stronger. Was she in love with him? How was she going to find the answer to that question? Where was it to be found?

"Jack Barlow," her father said, extending his hand to Declan. The two men shook hands. "I appreciate your understanding my feelings about Butch." He paused. "My daughter, it would seem, has forgotten her social manners."

"What?" Joy said, pulling herself from her own thoughts. "Oh, heavens, I didn't introduce you two. I'm sorry. Dad, when are we going to know more about Butch's condition?"

"Dr. Timbers is attempting to determine what kind of poison it is in order to know the proper treatment

. . . if there is any. It just seems to be taking forever, that's all. For a physician I'm certainly not behaving very well. I am what I believe is called a basket case. When I found Butch by the back fence in the yard, I . . ." Jack shook his head.

"Are you assuming that whatever contained the poison was thrown over the back fence?" Declan asked. "The poison had to have been in some kind of food that would be tempting to Butch."

"That's how I see it," Jack said. "Lord, I'd like to get my hands on whoever did this. What a senseless, vicious thing to do. I've got to warn the neighbors to be on the lookout for anyone going down the alley. The jerk may have gotten such a sick thrill from this, he'll decide to risk doing it again on the same street. I remember your explaining that mentality to me, Joy, when you were studying it in graduate school."

Declan looked quickly at Joy. "You studied the workings of the criminal mind?"

"Extensively," she said. "There are very often patterns of behavior that a trained psychologist or psychiatrist can chart, enabling the police to anticipate the person's next move."

"Oh." Declan frowned slightly. "I didn't realize that you . . . well, we'll get into that later. What concerns me now is the possibility that this wasn't a random choice, that the poisoned food was prepared specifically for Butch."

"Why on earth would anyone want to poison a lazy old dog who doesn't even bark unless the mood strikes?" Jack shook his head. "That doesn't make sense."

"I could be wrong, Dr. Barlow, but I didn't want to take any chances. So I reported the incident to—" The door opened and Vince strode in. "—him," Declan finished.

Declan remembered *his* social manners and introduced Vince to Joy and her father.

"Joy," Vince said. He shook her hand, but didn't release it. "I can't tell you what a sincere pleasure it is to meet you."

"Cut," Declan said, slicing one hand through the air. "Joy, ignore this pesky Italian. He gets extremely strange when in the presence of a beautiful woman."

Vince kissed the back of Joy's hand, then laughed when Declan punched him on the arm. Vince was serious again in the next moment and gave Jack Barlow a quick summary of what had been taking place.

"Dad," Joy said, "did you ask Bill Cooper what his opinion was about all of this when you were playing golf this afternoon?"

"Yes. He said he had to admit that the timing of Declan's apartment being ransacked was hard to call coincidental. He feels that it definitely points in Mildred Fairchild's direction. Bill really didn't want to discuss it further as it brings back painful memories of Jeff, so I just dropped it."

"Any clues yet as to where Mildred Fairchild is, Vince?" Declan asked.

"No. I've got a stakeout on her house in case she shows up. She seemed to disappear the moment she was released from the sanitarium. I've got clearance to talk to her, but I'll be damned if I can find her. Where do we stand here?"

"The vet is trying to determine what kind of poison was given to Butch," Joy said.

Vince nodded. "Good. I can use all the help I can get with this mess."

"You honestly believe this is connected to what happened to Declan?" Jack asked. "Butch was poisoned because he's my dog, I'm Joy's father, and Joy is seeing Declan? Isn't that a bit farfetched?"

"Not really, Dad," Joy said. "I thought Declan was overreacting at first too, but thinking back to my studies, I believe the theory is really on target. The boldness of the person's actions may indicate that he hopes to be caught and stopped. Or he has tunnel vision and is so desperate to complete his goals, he doesn't care about his own well-being. In other words, he'd be willing to die to accomplish what he's determined to do."

"Bingo," Vince said. "That's exactly what the police psychologist told me. The problem with that theory in this case is Mildred Fairchild's lack of time to gather information about Joy, Jack, and Butch. That bothers me."

"I see your point," Declan said. "She hasn't been out of the sanitarium long enough to put all of this together, has she? I sure don't think so."

"It's another piece to the puzzle," Vince said. "I read an article of yours, Joy, on women who commit violent crimes. You know what a rough road we're facing here trying to figure out Mildred Fairchild."

Declan stared at Joy. "No kidding? I had no idea that you had published articles. Why are you messing around with yuppies suffering from stress?"

Joy sighed. "Declan, my stress-management specialty is vitally important. Stress can kill, remember? I also use that specialty extensively when I'm working with Vietnam veterans in group therapy."

"You work with Vietnam vets?" he asked incredulously. "Those guys have been through hell. I didn't know you could help people like them."

"There's a hell of a lot you don't know, flake brain," Vince said gruffly, "but could we stick to the subject of the moment here? There's a crazy person out there who could possibly be widening his or her circle of those selected to pay for Jeff's death. Dr. Barlow, I'd like to send some lab people over to take a look at your yard and that alley."

"Yes, of course," Jack said.

"I don't expect to find a thing," Vince went on, "but I can't afford to pass up taking action on anything that might give us a clue to this joker's identity. I assume there isn't anyone you can think of offhand who would do this to your dog? An angry neighbor? A patient harboring a grudge because someone important to him died?"

Jack slowly shook his head. "I can't think of anyone. I'm retired now, I've known my neighbors for years . . . No, I'm afraid I can't be of any help."

"All right," Vince said. "If you think of something later, give me a call. I'll—"

The door to the examining rooms opened, and a young man with rust-colored hair and heavy glasses strode toward the group. "I did it," Dr. Timbers said, a wide smile breaking across his thin face. "We'll just see if my assistant kids me again about the mad-scientist lab I've set up in the back room. I isolated the poison given to Butch and have started him on the antidote."

"Oh, that's wonderful," Joy said. "Is Butch responding to the treatment?"

Dr. Timbers laughed. "He just beat the rhythm of 'De Camptown Races' with that wild tail of his. He's definitely on the mend."

"Thank God," Jack said, then cleared his throat roughly.

"I'd like to keep Butch here through the night," Dr. Timbers went on. "I'll be able to watch him, give him more of the antidote if he needs it, and I promise I'll hold his paw so he won't be homesick. He's asking for you, though, so you'd better go say hello. He's in the center room in the back."

"Come on, Dad," Joy said, grabbing her father's arm. "Thank you so much, Dr. Timbers."

"My pleasure," the veterinarian said. "Butch is a good old dog."

"Dr. Timbers," Vince said as Joy and Jack left to see Butch. "I'm Lieutenant Santini with the LAPD." He showed the veterinarian his badge. "What was the poison?"

"Metaldehyde, Lieutenant. It's used in products made to kill garden snails."

"Snails?" Declan said.

"They're a real nuisance in this area," Dr. Timbers explained. "The little buggers can gobble up an entire garden if you don't knock them out of there. This poison is very effective. It lures the snails to it and causes them to die of dehydration after they digest it. You can buy it anywhere that sells gardening supplies. By law there's a warning on it stating it's poisonous and could be fatal if consumed by children or pets."

"Wonderful," Vince muttered.

"So you're saying that anyone with a garden could have this stuff?" Declan asked.

"If they don't, they'll wish they did," Dr. Timbers said. "The snails are expected to be especially bad this year because we had so much rain in the spring. What the snails don't eat, the grasshoppers will, if the gardener doesn't do something to prevent it."

"I get the picture." Vince took a card from his

wallet and handed it to the doctor. "Would you call me if you think of anything else that might be helpful?"

Dr. Timbers glanced at the card. "Sure thing. I take it that this is more than just a poisoned dog you're investigating here?"

"I'm afraid so."

Joy returned from the back room and came to Declan's side. "Butch is doing so well," she said. "I can't thank you enough, Dr. Timbers. My father would like to stay awhile if that's all right."

"Sure. I'll be glad to have the company. Butch is a great one-man band with that tail of his, but he's not much on discussing the latest movies or best-selling books."

"I noticed that you removed Butch's collar," she said. "Should I take it with me now?"

Dr. Timbers frowned. "Butch wasn't wearing a collar when Dr. Barlow brought him in."

"I'll ask him if he took it off Butch when he found him in the yard," Vince said, and headed toward the back room.

"I'd better get back in there," Dr. Timbers said. "Good night, folks."

"Thanks again," Joy said.

Declan slipped his arm around her waist and pulled her close to him. He kissed her on the temple. "How are you doing?"

"I'm fine now, Declan. Thank you for coming with

me, and for understanding how upset my father was. You're a very thoughtful, caring man."

He grinned at her. "I'm sexy too."

"Indeed you are."

He leaned over and captured her lips with his.

"Hey! None of that stuff," Vince said, coming back into the front office. "Regulation four-fourteen-point-three-two states there will be no hanky-panky in veterinarians' offices. You're looking at a stiff fine, people."

"You're so full of bull, Santini," Declan said, rolling his eyes. Joy laughed. "A funny Italian cop. You'll be wanting your own TV series next."

"I'll give it some thought," Vince said. He paused. "No dog collar. Dr. Barlow didn't take it off Butch and didn't realize at the time that he wasn't wearing it. We'll check the yard at Dr. Barlow's house, but I doubt that it's there."

"Then where is it?" Joy asked.

"Ten bucks says it gets delivered to me at the station. Our charming friend will want to strut his—or her—stuff."

"That," Declan said, "is weird."

"You called it, Harris. I'll keep you posted. I've got to hit the road."

"It was wonderful meeting you," Joy said.

"Thanks for coming, Vince," Declan added.

"I never miss a party," Vince said. "Thanks for the invitation. See ya."

"He's a very nice man," Joy said, as Vince left the office.

"One of the best," Declan said. "Are you ready to go home?"

"Yes, I told my father we'd be leaving. I just realized how tired I am."

"Stress," Declan said. "You're suffering from stress. Trust me, I know about these things."

"Oh, put a cork in it," she said, starting toward the door.

Declan laughed and followed her out into the cool night. The sky was a silvery umbrella of stars. They walked slowly across the parking lot toward Declan's car.

"Declan," Joy said, suddenly stopping, "do you hear something? It's—it's an unusual but lovely sound, a sort of humming."

"Yes, I hear it now. Locusts?"

"No, I've never heard anything quite like this before. It's so . . . I can hardly describe it. It's soothing, comforting in some strange way. I wonder where—"

"Joy," Declan interrupted. "Look. Up in the sky. We forgot all about it because of rushing over here. There. See? It's the blue moon. The second full moon this month. See? It really is the blue moon!"

"I see it," Joy whispered. "The humming . . . Declan, it's louder now. Do you hear it?"

"Yes," he said, his gaze riveted to the sky.

Neither spoke further, nor hardly breathed, as they stared up at the heavens, at the rising blue moon. It seemed to grow bigger and brighter, and the strange, lovely humming continued. The parking lot and all beyond it disappeared.

A warmth consumed Joy, filling her with a sense of peace and contentment. She looked at the glowing blue moon, and a soft smile touched her lips. It was a womanly smile, a knowing smile, a serene smile.

She was in love with Declan Harris.

It was suddenly as clear to her as the bright, silvery blue moon. The confusion was gone, the answer found.

She loved him.

Declan blinked, assured himself that the blue moon was actually there, and listened intently to the comforting humming. He felt warm, he realized, but it was a heat that came from within and was pleasant, not uncomfortable.

The blue moon, he mused. He was really seeing it in all its splendor with the woman he loved.

He stiffened, shot a quick glance at Joy, then stared at the blue moon again.

He was in love with Joy Barlow! He really was. There were no more doubts, no more questions. He knew he loved her. And it felt terrific.

"Joy," he whispered. "The Legend of the Blue Moon says . . ."

"I know," she murmured. "I didn't believe in legends, in fairy tales, but now . . ."

"Joy?"

They turned to each other at the same moment, their eyes meeting, searching, and finding what they now knew to be true.

"I love you, Joy Barlow. I really do."

"And I love you, Declan Harris. Oh yes, Declan, I do love you so very much."

His hands cupped her face, then he kissed her gently, reverently, as though sealing their commitment with the blue moon as a witness.

It was a moment like none they had ever known, filled with unspoken promises and paths of sunshine they would travel down together. It was a moment of tomorrows that stretched into infinity. It was a moment of love.

Slowly the humming faded, then disappeared, but the warmth within Joy and Declan remained. They were aware once more of where they were, of the sounds of the city and the night surrounding them. It was as though they'd been transported to a faraway place and had safely returned, but were changed for all time.

"Let's go home," Declan said quietly.

"Yes, Declan," Joy said, "let's go home."

They exchanged another warm smile, then, arms around each other, they walked the remaining distance to the car. Neither spoke as Declan drove out of the parking lot.

"Joy," he said finally, "I've decided that I was wrong about us not seeing each other. Now that this has happened to Butch, it puts things in a different light."

"Good," she said. "I was getting tired of that argument. We'll just drop the subject."

"Well, no, not exactly," he said slowly.

"Not exactly?"

"I'm adopting an opposite view, as a matter of fact." He shot her a quick grin, then redirected his attention to his driving. "I think we should stay very close to each other."

"Oh?" she said, raising her eyebrows.

"Let's discuss this when we get to your place. I need all my concentration for driving in this traffic."

"*Mmm,*" she said, staring at him with narrowed eyes.

In Joy's apartment Declan drew her into his arms and kissed her very thoroughly. Her knees were trembling when he released her, and she quickly sat down on the sofa. Declan settled next to her and picked up one of her hands. He placed it on his thigh and kept it covered with his.

Heat from Declan's muscled thigh immediately swept up Joy's arm and tingled through her body. She shifted slightly to face him, but when she attempted to pull her hand free, his grip tightened.

"Now then," he said, "let's get this over with. It's really very simple. I love you, you love me, you're in possible danger because of me, so I'm going to protect you. I'll do that by moving in here with you until this mess is cleared up."

"What!"

"Or you can move in with me. I'm a reasonable, easy-to-get-along-with kind of guy. You can decide which plan suits your fancy. Plan A or B? Your wish is my command."

She jumped to her feet and planted her fists on her hips. "My wish, Mr. Harris, is to tell you where you can put your ridiculous plans. This is absurd. I'm not taking up residency with you on a whim. *Maybe* I'm in danger. *Maybe* Mildred Fairchild is behind all of this. And on that kind of flimsy evidence, I'm supposed to set up housekeeping with you, live with you? Ha! If and when I ever decide to live with a man, sir, that decision will be made with my heart, not my head. And certainly not some harebrained Plan A or B. You have a lot of gall, do you know that?"

Declan also got to his feet. "You're not being reasonable. You could be in danger, dammit. And besides, it's not as if we haven't already slept"—Joy narrowed her eyes and pursed her lips—"together," he finished weakly. "Harris, you're in trouble." He dragged a hand through his hair.

"You're leaving is what you are," Joy said tightly.

"That's Plan C. Good night, Declan. It's been fascinating talking to you. You may now exit stage left."

He crossed his arms over his chest. "No."

"No? This is my home. I want you to go. You can't say 'No.' "

"I just did. And I will again. No. I'm not leaving you alone, Joy. I love you, remember? Whoever is behind these incidents is getting bolder, and I'm not taking any chances that something might happen to you. I'll go crazy pacing the floor at my place."

"Well, I'd be worried about you too, Declan. If we're together . . . I have a feeling I'm going to run out of reasonable reasons as to why I won't do this." She paused. "I give up. Yes, all right, I agree. You should move in here."

"Thank you, my love." He brushed his lips over hers. "Joy, we owe it to the blue moon to concentrate on each other now. I want to make love to you."

She sighed. "I want you too, Declan."

He lifted her into his arms and carried her into the bedroom.

Their lovemaking was slow and sensuous, each wishing to anticipate for as long as possible that moment of ecstasy when they flew beyond reality.

They touched and kissed, explored the mysteries of his hard body and her soft one, teased and tantalized with lips and hands. They murmured endearments, declared their love over and over, and when passion's heat threatened to consume them, they became one at last.

They were in love and making love, and it was a night of magic. When they scaled the heights of passion, they were together. And together still, they drifted gently back to the here and now.

They lay sated and content, heads resting on the same pillow, bodies close, hands entwined.

"The Legend of the Blue Moon," Joy murmured. "It was such a beautiful moon, Declan, so big and bright, glowing like a silvery ball."

"It was spectacular all right. Joy, the legend . . . do you believe in it now? Lord knows I do. I was so confused, asking myself every other second if I was really in love with you, wondering how I was going to find out, be sure. Then when I saw the blue moon, I knew that I loved you."

"Everything you just said was true for me too. My mind was all muddled, but when I stood there gazing up at the blue moon . . . I love you, Declan. The scientific part of my mind says there are no such things as fairy tales and legends, but the woman part of me knows how I felt when I saw the blue moon."

He kissed her on the forehead. "We, together, have our blue moon and its legend. I suppose it's corny, but I really like knowing that the blue moon is ours."

"Yes, I like it too." She paused. "Declan, we love each other, but . . . well, that doesn't automatically make things perfect for us."

"I know that. Every couple has kinks they have to work out because they're individuals. I assure you, ma'am, that I don't squeeze the toothpaste tube in the middle. That can be a big problem, you know. Relationships have been known to crash and burn over toothpaste tubes. 'Get out of my face, you scum, you squeezed the toothpaste in the middle again.'"

"Declan, I'm serious. My concern is your attitude about my career. I've known from the moment we met that you don't really respect what I do, what I've chosen as my profession, what is very important to me. You heard some things in the veterinarian's office tonight that obviously surprised you."

"Yes, that's true. I didn't realize that being a psychologist covered as much territory as it does. You know, your working with Vietnam vets, your theories matching up with what the police shrink had told Vince . . . but . . ."

"But?"

"Lord, Joy, do we have to get into this tonight? This is our night, ours and the blue moon's. We've discovered that we're in love with each other, we've just made incredibly beautiful love together. Let's go to sleep concentrating on each other and our love, okay? We'll tackle the rest of it, work everything out. You'll see. But not tonight, okay?

"All right," she said softly. "This is a very special night. Everything else can wait . . . for now."

"Good." He kissed her deeply. "Sleep well, my love."

"You too. I love you, Declan."

"I love you very, very much, Joy."

Within minutes Declan's steady breathing told Joy he was asleep. She stared up into the darkness, knowing peaceful slumber would not come to her that easily.

She had to be patient, she told herself. Declan was slowly seeing her career in greater depth, learning that she was more than just another fad. It would all become clear to him in time, and time was what was called for, along with the patience she had to muster.

She yawned, then snuggled closer to him, savoring his heat and the strength in his powerful body. Oh, heavens, how she loved this man, and how glorious to know that he loved her.

"Thank you, blue moon," she whispered to the darkness, then drifted off to sleep.

Eight

By midafternoon on Monday, Joy had a headache that felt like a hundred little drummer boys beating against her temples. She swallowed two aspirin, leaned back in her desk chair, and closed her eyes.

A tension headache, she thought with disgust. A crummy stress-induced headache that she'd allowed to get the better of her. She'd done relaxing breathing exercises, had envisioned herself on the quiet shores of a deserted beach with the ocean waves lapping gently up and over her legs. But the drummers beat on, her head pounding with increasing pain.

She was angry at herself not only for allowing stress to dictate to her personal comfort, but also because she knew the source of that stress—Declan.

It was as though there were two Joy Barlows oper-ating on different planes within her own body and mind, she mused. One was aglow with happiness over discovering that she was truly in love for the first time, and loved in return by the man of her heart.

That Joy had spent a lazy, lovemaking Sunday with Declan, focusing only on him and the glorious hours they shared. They'd closed out the world, al-lowing only the magic of the blue moon to enter their private haven.

Then there was the other Joy. That one had hov-ered just below the surface of her happiness and contentment, prodding her, insisting that she sit Declan down and discuss at length his attitudes toward her profession.

She'd attempted to broach the subject a few times, only to be silenced by Declan's searing kiss that had caused her to totally forget what she had been about to say. After her third try she'd known without a doubt that Declan was not prepared to discuss the matter during the stolen hours of their glorious Sunday.

And so the stress had brewed beneath the surface of her mind, hidden behind her smile, to show itself today in the form of a raging headache.

Tonight, she decided, they were going to talk this through. They had to.

She stood and walked slowly to the fish tank. She

watched the lazy back-and-forth swimming of the fish and didn't move until James informed her that her next patient had arrived. With a weary sigh she forced a smile onto her lips and realized that the drummers in her head hadn't slowed their maddening cadence one bit.

Declan looked up from the drafting board as a short man in his mid-thirties entered the office.

"Here you go, Declan," the man said. "Clara and I have the preliminary drawings for the nursing home project ready for your inspection."

"Roll them out here, Tim," Declan said, pushing aside his pencils and pens. Tim whipped the tube of paper flat onto the board and anchored the edges with a pencil holder, a paperweight, and his elbows. Declan scanned the intricate drawing. "Looks good," he said, nodding. "Excellent."

"I've got the scale in my pocket if you'll hold this corner," Tim said. "I know you want to check the measurements."

"That won't be necessary," Declan said. "You and Clara have never been off a millimeter in the past, so there's no reason to think there's anything wrong with this."

"You're kidding," Tim said.

"Nope. It's called delegating, trusting the people I searched high and low for to do the job I hired them to do. Delegating reduces stress, Timothy my man. I have fallen prey to stress, and I'm correcting the error of my ways."

"Oh, good Lord," Tim said, laughing, "you sound like my wife. She's driving me nuts with dissertations on that stuff. I wish she'd go back to her 'Save the Wildlife' crusade. This latest phase of quoting her psychologist every two minutes is bugging the hell out of me."

Declan frowned. "Oh?"

"Mary Lou, my wife, announced at dinner last night that she was not just Tim's wife and Jeremy's mother, she was a person, a woman. I told her that I didn't think she was an Irish setter, for crying out loud, and she threw a glop of mashed potatoes at me. Ready for this? I don't understand who she is, what her inner needs are. Cripes. I love her, can't imagine my life without her. What does she want from me? I wish to hell she'd never started going to the shrink. A couple of her friends were seeing the guy, and Mary Lou jumped on the bandwagon. For seventy-five dollars an hour I'm getting nothing but grief when I walk in my front door at night. There ought to be a law against those shrinks who fill women's heads with that garbage. Don't you agree, Declan?"

"Well, I . . ."

"I know you do, because you said so when you were dating Ginger what's-her-name. You said Ginger couldn't carry on a conversation without stopping every few minutes to meditate, or whatever the hell she did, because her analyst told her to maintain her inner peace at all times. What a bunch of bull; and they charge a bundle to dish out malarkey like that." He paused. "Well, I didn't mean to go on about that. It's just that I've had it with Mary Lou and this latest trip of hers. Thanks for the go-ahead on these plans, Declan. I'll tell Clara that we're ready to roll." He picked up the blueprints and left the room.

Declan watched Tim leave, then ran his hands down his face. Dammit, he thought, he could have gone ten years without hearing what Tim had just said.

He slid off the stool and walked to his floor-to-ceiling window. Bracing his hands on the glass, he stared down at the surging traffic below.

He loved Joy, and she loved him. The hours they'd spent together since they'd seen the blue moon had been fantastic, and he'd never forget them. He wanted to shout from the rooftops how much he loved Joy Barlow. The woman.

And Dr. Joy Barlow?

Dammit, Declan fumed, he was trying to get a handle on his attitude about Joy's career. But apparently he was expected to change all his views on the subject of psychologists, analysts, therapists, the whole group. There was no compromise being offered here, no middle of the road. He either went the whole distance, or forgot it.

He'd begun this day with a firm determination to shape up his act, toss out old prejudices and view things with a fresh and open mind. He'd been doing fairly well until Tim had arrived with his tale of woe.

"Damn," he muttered, pushing himself away from the window.

Joy was going to square off on this issue, and it would probably be tonight, he surmised. He had a knot in his gut and a worsening headache that said the discussion wasn't going to go well at all. He refused to lie to her, and what he had to say wasn't what she wanted to hear. He loved her, dammit. Why couldn't that be enough? Why wasn't Declan, the man and his love, enough?

His phone rang, bringing him from his tangled thoughts. He crossed the room and snatched up the receiver."

"Yes?"

"Vince Santini on line one," his secretary said.

"Thanks." He pressed the flashing button. "Vince? How's life among the grime and slime?"

"Cute," Vince said. "As a matter of fact, I have some interesting news which I may now choose not to share with you. Grime and slime? Is that any way to talk about the grime and slime who roam the streets of our fair city? Shame on you."

Declan laughed. "I beg your humble pardon, Lieutenant. What's your news flash?"

Vince's voice was serious when he spoke again. "Butch's collar arrived right on schedule. It was found in a large envelope on a bench in the reception area, my name on it in those cut-out letters again. The bomb boys had to do their thing first, but I knew it was the dog's collar."

"Any note?"

"Nope. I also have interesting news about Mildred Fairchild."

"Oh?" Declan sat down in the chair behind his desk.

"The doctor from the sanitarium called me. He'd heard from Mildred's sister, Linda, in Florida. Linda said her mother-in-law had had a heart attack and she and her husband had to fly to Chicago. She had no choice but to ask Mildred to postpone her trip to Florida. Linda has been back for three days and can't reach Mildred by phone at any time during the day or night. She's very concerned about her."

"You're saying that Mildred never left LA?"

"So it would seem. I've requested a search warrant to enter her house to look for evidence that she's been in there, plus to see if I find any of that poison used on Butch. Mildred hasn't been seen near the place since I've had a stakeout on it."

"Do you think you can get the search warrant?"

"I'm going to raise the roof if I don't. I have just cause, and I've filled out their fancy request forms in triplicate. The thing that blows my mind about these warrants is that it's so damn subjective. If it lands in front of a judge who had a fight with his wife at breakfast, he's liable to refuse any request at all. It gets down to his opinion versus mine, with his mood thrown in to muddy the waters. Lousy system, Declan, no doubt about it. I need to get inside that house. Between you and me, chum, I *intend* to get inside that house."

"Wonderful," Declan said dryly. "A police lieutenant arrested for breaking and entering."

"I gotta do what I gotta do."

"Vince, you're asking to get booted right off the force. I know you get tired of the red tape and politics, but don't go nuts about it."

"We'll see. Listen, stay as close to Joy as possible, Declan. I have such bad vibes about this whole thing. I don't know, it's just not fitting together right in my mind. Something is off kilter, and I can't quite put my finger on it."

"Believe me, I'm hardly letting Joy out of my sight. Vince, I— I love her. I'm really honest-to-God in love with her. And she loves me."

"Hey, that's terrific, and I'm happy for you, I truly am. Joy is a classy lady. Why she picked a screwball like you I don't know, but we'll allow her a flaw or two. Speaking of flaws, Harris, did you get your head on straight yet about Joy's career?"

"I'm trying, Vince, but all I end up doing is chasing arguments around in my head and not getting anything concrete to hold on to. I learn something positive, then have two negative facts reinforced."

"Not good."

"There's a part of me that's getting ticked off too. Why do I have to change my opinion on this one hundred percent? What about compromise?"

"On this issue? No way. That's like saying to someone that they should settle for being sort of pregnant. It's all or nothing, Declan. You accept and respect Joy's career, or get out of the relationship and her life."

"Hell."

"That's the bottom line, brother. I've got to go. I'll keep you posted on Mildred Fairchild and whatever else surfaces about this fiasco. In the meantime watch your back and look after your lady."

"Guaranteed. Thanks for bringing me up to date, Vince. I'll talk to you later. Bye."

Declan slowly replaced the receiver and squeezed the bridge of his nose.

Lord, his head was killing him. He'd concentrate on something other than the increasing pain.

His glance fell on a small envelope on top of the mail scattered on his desk. He opened it, sliding out a card with a picture of a bubbling glass of champagne on the front. He flipped it open and read what was inside.

"I'll be damned," he said.

• • •

Joy entered her apartment, slipped off her shoes, and sat down on the sofa with a sigh. Her headache was no better, she realized, as she sifted through her mail. She wanted to take a leisurely bubble bath, have a cup of tea, and crawl into bed.

But Declan would be arriving any minute, and to postpone what she knew she must discuss with him would be foolish. The problem wasn't going to go away by ignoring it. Tonight, headache or not, they were going to talk it through.

She heard Declan's key in the door just as she found a small envelope among the bills and advertisements in her mail.

"Hi," she said, smiling at him.

"Hi." He crossed the room and dropped a quick kiss on her lips. "How are you?"

"Okay, except for a stinky headache." She opened the envelope.

"This must be the day for headaches. I have a beaut too."

"A champagne glass?" Joy said, looking at the card. She opened it and smiled. "Oh, Declan, this is really wonderful."

He pulled his matching card from his jacket pocket. "I got one too. What's the big deal? Bill Cooper is having a cocktail party tomorrow night at eight o'clock. It surprised me at first, but then I remembered that he always did like to entertain."

"That's why it's wonderful, don't you see? This is

the first social event Bill has planned since Jeff was killed."

Declan ran his fingers over his throbbing forehead. He could literally feel the simmering anger within him gaining force, inching its way toward the surface. He struggled for patience, for an inner calm that flitted just beyond his reach.

"Yes," Joy said decisively, "this is a very positive sign. It could be a turning point for Bill, the signal that he is, at long last, taking the tentative steps to put his grief to rest."

The pounding in Declan's head increased as his anger soared. "For God's sake, Joy, do you have to analyze everything everyone does? We're talking about a couple of drinks and some cheese and crackers here. But that means Bill is making great emotional breakthroughs regarding his grieving process for his dead son?"

"Declan, what—"

"Try this one," he interrupted. "I put on my right sock, then my right shoe. Left sock, then left shoe. Most people put on both their socks, then their shoes. So, O Mighty Shrink, what chapter in the textbook is that in? What nifty little gems do you now have to fling at me about my inner self because of the way I put on my socks and shoes? Well? Lay it on me."

Joy could feel the blood drain from her face. "It's all a joke to you, isn't it? My profession, my career.

That part of who I am is just a joke to you. In spite of what you heard in the veterinarian's office, you haven't budged an inch. You think I'm playing games with people who are bored." She stood on trembling legs, fighting back her tears.

"I'm trying, dammit!" he roared. "I'm trying to get a handle on what you do, but it won't come together for me. What about who I am when I walk through that door at the end of the day, the fact that I'm the man who loves you? Doesn't that count for anything? No, I don't think it does. I'm on borrowed time as you wait and watch for signals that say I'm accepting you as a psychologist as well as a woman. I have to do all the changing, or it's the end of our relationship. Dammit, I love you. That sure as hell ought to be worth something."

"Dear Lord, Declan, listen to yourself. The man who loves me. Yes, the total man, who is proud of what he's accomplished. You wouldn't be the Declan Harris I know if you considered yourself a failure, if your self-esteem was in constant shreds, if—"

"Quit doing your shrink routine on me."

"I'm not! I'm simply trying to make you understand that we are complete entities formed by all that we've done, seen, learned. You can't peel away layers of people like dealing cards from a deck, deciding which to keep and which to throw away. You love Joy Barlow the woman, but I wouldn't be that woman if I weren't also a psychologist. Dear heaven,

Declan, can't you see that? Love is absolute, total, accepting all and everything about the other person." She nearly choked on a sob. "Oh, Declan, can't you see that?"

"God, I don't know, I can't think." He pressed the heels of his hands to his temples. "Why isn't my loving you enough? Why in the hell does love have to be this complicated?" He dragged one hand through his hair. "I need some time alone, I guess. Hell, I don't know." He turned and started toward the door.

"Declan, no, don't go," Joy said, wiping tears from her cheeks. "We can't solve this if we don't sort it through together. Everything we have is at stake."

He yanked open the door. "Do you think I don't realize that? I love you, Joy, but what I can't deal with is the fact that my love, myself, isn't enough for you. That's it. I've had it for tonight. Keep the door locked and don't let anyone in. Vince is pretty convinced that Mildred Fairchild is in the area. I'll be back later to make sure you're okay. Don't wait up."

"Declan, please, don't—"

He left the apartment and slammed the door behind him.

"Oh, Declan," Joy murmured. "I love you so much. We'll find the answers. We will. Declan?"

She stumbled across the room and into the bedroom where she flung herself onto the bed and cried, her sobs seeming to tear at her very soul.

The sad sound echoed in the room, drowning out

the quiet humming that might have soothed at least some of the pain of her shattering heart.

Declan entered his office, reached automatically for the lights, then hesitated. He shoved his hands into his pockets, leaving the room in darkness, and made his way across the room to the windows. He pulled open the drapes and stared moodily down, the cars appearing like children's toys inching along the street below.

He didn't want to be standing there alone in his office with a throbbing headache and a burning stomach. He wanted to be with Joy. Holding her, kissing her, making love with her. But he'd stormed out in anger and frustration, and the price he was paying was a solitary stretch of hours in his office.

He glanced around the room, at the silhouettes of the furniture, and realized that this room and all it represented was no longer enough. He and Jeff had concentrated most of their energies here, then Declan had doubled his efforts when Jeff was killed. He'd done his part, and Jeff's, to ensure that Harris and Cooper made it to the top and stayed there. He owed that to Jeff because . . .

Declan swore under his breath and turned to stare once again out the window.

Joy, he remembered, had insisted that he didn't owe Jeff a debt, that Jeff had been responsible for his own actions. If that was really true, then Declan had no reason to work himself to the brink of exhaustion. He could bring in a new partner and start living a balanced life again, and have many hours to share with Joy.

Joy. Joy the woman and Joy the psychologist. A package deal. Accept both, or hit the road. Hell.

The clouds in the sky suddenly parted and there, as if it knew Declan would be its audience, was the blue moon. As he looked at it, he thought he heard that strange humming sound again. Then he forgot about that as he allowed himself to savor the memories of all he had shared with Joy.

"Well, buddy," he said to the moon, "do you have any answers for me? I'm in love, and here I stand alone and lonely."

The moon seemed to glow more brightly as Declan continued to gaze at it, losing all track of time.

She was, Joy decided sullenly, sick to death of staring at fish. There she stood in her swanky office, Ms. Psychologist Extraordinaire, gawking at a bunch of round-eyed creatures that did nothing more than swim back and forth, opening and closing their mouths. It wasn't relaxing, it was ridiculous.

She knew darn well that those fish weren't going to solve her problems with Declan, nor were they going to make her forget the long, miserable night she'd spent in her bed without him. She'd heard him enter the apartment hours after he'd left, but he hadn't come into the bedroom. Exhaustion had finally claimed her as she'd pictured him stretched out on the sofa, and when she'd awakened at dawn he was already gone.

Oh, Declan, she thought, wrapping her arms around herself and fighting against fresh tears. She loved him so much, wanted to be with him every spare minute they had. Laughing, talking, making plans, making love. She wanted . . .

Joy stiffened, staring blindly at the fish tank.

She wanted . . . she wanted . . . she wanted . . .

The words beat against her brain as a cold, tight fist curled around her heart.

Physician heal thyself, she thought miserably, because there it was, the answer.

She was possibly facing a future of being alone and lonely, perhaps having lost the love of Declan Harris, because she had demanded that their relationship be perfect. Demanded that it be exactly the way she wanted it to be.

Declan was to shape up or get out.

And last night he had walked away, defeated, tired, confused, because she told him he didn't measure up. He had tried, he'd said, to understand and come to grips with her career. He had attempted to get a handle on it, accept and respect it as she had so adamantly stated he should.

Dr. Joy Marilee Barlow, she fumed at herself, just who in the blue blazes do you think you are?

"Oh, Lord," she said, shaking her head. Had she even once asked Declan about his career? No. Had she inquired about his struggle up the ladder of success, what it had taken him to reach the level of prestige he now had? No. Had she discovered which buildings, which homes had been designed by him? No.

She'd been too busy telling Declan what *she wanted.*

And in the middle of one of her tantrums, Declan had walked out the door.

And out of her life?

Oh no, please no, Joy thought frantically. She'd been so wrong, so demanding and wrong. There was so much she could tell him about her work that he didn't know, a multitude of examples of the good she'd done that would counteract the evidence he had of the flip side of the coin.

Joy glared at the fish in the tank. "Close your mouths, for pete's sake," she said aloud. "You look like idiots." She walked slowly to her desk and settled into the leather chair.

Time, she mused. Declan needed time and patience to have a chance to truly understand her profession. And he would have all the time he needed, coupled with infinite patience. She would match his efforts with her own as she explored and discovered all there was to know about Harris and Cooper, Architects. They would do it together, step by step.

If it wasn't too late.

She drew a shuddering breath and swallowed past the ache of tears in her throat. Glancing at her watch, she saw it was nearly five o'clock. It had been a long, hideous day, during which she'd had difficulty pulling her mind from Declan and concentrating on her patients.

When would she see him again? she wondered. Would he come to her apartment after work? No, why should he walk into a room where he knew unreasonable demands were going to be made of him?

She jerked in her chair as her telephone rang, bringing her from her tangled and tormented thoughts. She pressed the blinking button and lifted the receiver.

"Yes, James?"

"Mr. Harris is here. You don't have any more appointments today. Shall I tell him to come to your office?"

Declan was there? she thought, her mind racing. He'd come? Why? To say good-bye forever? No!

"Hello?"

"Oh yes, of course, James, tell Mr. Harris to come into my office. Thank you." She replaced the receiver with a shaking hand. Declan was there.

"Joy."

Her head snapped up and her heart pounded hard at the sight of him in the doorway. He looked magnificent. And very tired.

"Declan, I . . ." She stood, willing her knees not to buckle.

She wished she wasn't wearing her dark, tailored "power suit" with a pristine white blouse. She'd grabbed the first thing her hand had touched that morning when she'd gotten dressed, but now regretted her choice. She wanted to look feminine and pretty, so it would be Joy the woman who was speaking to Declan.

He moved into the office and closed the door behind him. She came out from behind her desk, and they both stopped, a room apart.

"I have to talk to you," Declan said, his voice low. "I'm not here to discuss my stress level." He unbuttoned his jacket and shoved his hands into his trouser pockets.

"Yes, I have to talk to you too," Joy said, hearing the unsteadiness in her own voice. She waved one hand in the air. "Would you like to sit down?"

"No."

"Oh." She took a step backward to lean against her desk. "Declan, I—"

"*I* came to *you*," he said, interrupting her. "That gives me the right to speak first, don't you think?"

"Yes, of course. Go ahead."

"I shouldn't have left you alone last night, Joy,

and I'm sorry about that. I assured Vince that I would be watching over you, and I did a lousy job of it."

"I was fine, Declan. I don't need a baby-sitter," she said quietly, searching his face for some clue as to what he was thinking. She found none.

"Still, I should have stayed with you." He paused to draw in a deep breath, then let it out slowly. "I did a lot of thinking last night with the blue moon for company. My mind was bouncing all over the place like a Ping-Pong ball, and it settled for a while on my parents, what it was like at home when I was a kid. My dad was a city bus driver, and my mom worked in a jewelry store."

He pulled his hands from his pockets and dragged restless fingers through his hair. "Those aren't very fancy jobs, are they? But every night at dinner they'd share stories about who they'd seen during the day. Lord, I loved those stories. I think they pepped them up a bit sometimes for me, but dinner was my favorite time of day. My dad told about the people who got on his bus—there was a guy with two body-guards once, on a bus, if you can believe that—and my mother waited on a movie star, a beautiful actress who bought a huge emerald ring to match a new dress. They had hundreds of stories, and I loved every one of them. I realize now that they truly respected each other and the careers they'd each chosen."

"Declan . . ."

"Please, let me finish. I pictured us, Joy, at the end of the day sitting down to dinner. What do we say to each other beyond commenting on the weather? If I suggest we go for a drive to see a building I designed, you wouldn't know what I was talking about. If you said you'd made an unhappy teenager smile, I wouldn't understand what the big deal was. So, we do what? Keep looking at our watches until it's time for bed and we can make love, because that's the only way we're really close, really able to express how much we love each other? It's not enough, is it?"

She shook her head. "No."

"Joy, after I left you last night, I realized that I wanted you to know about Harris and Cooper, Architects, how Jeff and I got started, nearly starved but hung in there. I want to take you out and say, 'See? Look at that building. I designed that one, and now it's real, and people work in there.' And oh, God, Joy, I want to understand what you do here all day. I know there's more to it than flakes like me who work too hard and stress themselves out. More to it than bored housewives on a new kick."

"Oh, yes, Declan, much more."

"And somewhere in the middle of the night it hit me like a brick right between the eyes. You took the time and energy, used your expertise and managed to give to me, like a gift-wrapped present, my life.

You saw, understood, and explained to me that I was working so hard out of misplaced guilt about what happened to Jeff. I heard you, but I didn't listen . . . until last night. I can see it all now so clearly. You, Joy, the psychologist, have turned things around for me. Respect you? Lord, I can't begin to tell you how much. I respect and love *all* of you, Joy Barlow. I swear I do."

"Oh, Declan," she whispered, tears filling her eyes.

"You're so warm and caring, and when we make love, you give of yourself totally, holding nothing back from me. You dropped everything and ran when your father was upset about Butch, and you didn't hesitate to express your feelings for a special, old dog."

He shoved his hands back into his pockets.

"Because that's who you are," he went on. "You're all that and more, the woman I fell in love with. You care, and you love, with everything you possess within you. And that's what you give to me *and* to your patients, right? Am I right, Joy?"

"Oh yes, Declan, yes," she said, her voice choked with emotion. "You're trying so hard to understand what I do and that it's a part of who I am. I didn't give you enough time, didn't have enough patience. I demanded what I wanted, then became hurt and angry when you couldn't do it on my timetable. Oh, Declan, I'm so sorry, and I was so wrong, and I hope you'll forgive me. I love you very much. We have endless things to bring to each other, and I want to share all of your world and all of mine. We'll learn it step by step, everything. Then, when we make love, it will mean even more to us because we'll both be joining with a person we know and love as well as we know ourselves. Declan, can we start over? I made terrible mistakes, but I'm asking you for another chance."

"I'm the one who messed up," he said, his voice suddenly raspy. "I was in love for the first time in my life, and I resented that it should be so damn complicated. I'd waited a long time to find you, and I didn't want anything muddying the waters. We'll just love each other, I figured, and the hell with the rest of the stuff. And I got angry because I couldn't see why my love wasn't enough for you. Well, it isn't, I know that now. I'm Declan Harris, of Harris and Cooper, Architects, and you're Dr. Joy Barlow, Psychologist, and that's part of who we are. I was dense, stubborn, and I'm so damn sorry. *I'm* the one who's asking for another chance, and for your forgiveness. I love you, Joy, all of you."

"Oh, Declan."

He pulled his hands free and held out his arms to her. "Come here, or I'll come there, or something, but I need you close to me, with me. Oh Joy, I don't want to lose you."

She ran across the room and flung herself into his arms with such force, he staggered before wrapping his arms tightly around her. She circled his back with her own arms and buried her face in the curve of his neck, trying to stop her flow of tears.

Seconds ticked away and they didn't move. They simply clung to each other, holding fast, feeling the chill of loneliness within them replaced once more by the warmth of love. They had come so close, so frighteningly close to losing, and the knowledge of their victory was sweeter for having fought a tough battle and won. They had a great deal more to learn about each other and about love, but they would do it, step by step, together.

The warmth slowly changed to the heat of desire, kindling the embers of passion within them. Joy lifted her head and Declan lowered his, finding her lips, seeking her tongue in the darkness of her mouth.

The kiss was rough at first, forcing into oblivion the memories of tears, of loneliness, of misery. And then the kiss gentled as hearts raced and breathing quickened.

Joy's breasts seemed to swell, longing for his touch. She pressed against him, savoring his heat, the evidence of his arousal. Her skin tingled with sensual awareness, and a liquid fire flowed through her, sparking her passion.

Declan could feel his control slipping as his body tightened, his manhood heavy and aching to be sheathed in the welcoming heat of Joy's body. His fear of losing her had been put to rest, and the future was theirs. He wanted to make love to her, to seal their commitment with the beautiful, intimate act that would reaffirm the promise of tomorrows shared.

He lifted his head and met her smoky gaze.

"I want you," he said. "I want to make love to you." He smiled. "But not here, because those fish are staring at us and this is none of their business."

She smiled too. "They're too young to know about these things, anyway." Her smile faded. "And I want you, Declan. Let's leave here, go home together. Oh, how I love you."

"I love you too, and before this night is over, we'll have a serious discussion about getting married, whether we want four, five, or six kids, stuff like that. But first things first . . . you, me, making love. And yes, I really do love you. That old blue moon outdid itself when it knocked me over with that news flash."

"The blue moon, our private, wonderful legend. We'll tell our two children all about the blue moon someday."

"Yes, and—two kids? That's all?"

She laughed. "Why don't we have them one at a time and see how it goes?"

"Fair enough. Can we get out of here now?"

"Yes, sir. Oh, Declan, I just remembered. We're supposed to go to Bill Cooper's cocktail party tonight."

"Not until eight o'clock. We have plenty of time before we have to go over there. Plenty of time to make love, my love, if we quit talking about it and get on with it. Do I sound like a sex maniac?"

"Yes, and I'm delighted. Let's not waste any more time standing here."

A rather confused but extremely interested James watched Joy and Declan pass his desk, Declan's arm around Joy's shoulders. She waggled her fingers at James, told him to have a pleasant evening, then the pair left the office. James smiled.

Declan closed the door to Joy's apartment, shutting out the world beyond it, and reached for the woman he loved, who moved eagerly into his embrace.

They were together, and it was ecstasy beyond their wildest dreams.

Nine

Joy watched Declan comb his hair as she tucked her blue silk blouse into white linen slacks, and a soft smile touched her lips. This was like being married, she thought dreamily, as she settled at her dressing table to brush her hair. They'd made beautiful love together, then showered and dressed for Bill's cocktail party. And it all felt so incredibly right.

"Leave your hair loose, all right?" Declan said, coming up behind her. He placed his hands on her shoulders and leaned over so that their faces were reflected side by side in the mirror. "Will you?"

She met his gaze in the mirror and smiled. "Of course. I prefer it that way myself, instead of twisted so tightly in a bun. Maybe I should cut it."

"No! Don't even think such a thing. Your hair is gorgeous. When it's sliding over me when we're . . ." He straightened and cleared his throat. "Yes, well, I don't think this is the time to be discussing . . . what I started to discuss."

Joy's laughter was interrupted by the ringing of the telephone. She crossed the room and picked up the receiver.

"Hello?"

"Dr. Barlow?"

"Yes."

"This is the security guard in the building where you have your office. That fancy fish tank of yours isn't bubbling like usual. I figured I'd best tell you that it's not working right."

She frowned. "Oh, well, thank you. I appreciate your being so conscientious."

"You'll come fix it, then?"

"Yes, I'll be right over."

"Fine. Bye."

"Good-bye," she said, and slowly replaced the receiver. "That's strange."

"Problem?" Declan asked.

"Not really. The fish tank in my office isn't working properly. It's no doubt due for a new stone in the filter system. It will take only a minute to replace, and I have a box of spares there. What's strange is that the security guard called. I wasn't aware the security guards had keys to the private offices."

"The manager or owner of the building must have told you, Joy. I can't imagine them giving authority to someone to go into the private offices without informing the tenants. Besides, they'd want to rave about that perk to justify your hefty rent."

She shrugged. "It isn't important, I guess. The fact remains that we need to stop by my office on the way to Bill's house so that I can fix the filter."

"Your chariot awaits, madame." Declan pulled her into his arms and kissed her deeply. "Ready?" he asked, when he finally released her.

Joy nodded, knowing that no words would come if she attempted to speak. On legs that were definitely trembling, she followed Declan from the room.

In the lobby of the office building, Joy glanced around. "I don't see the security guard."

Declan chuckled. "That's the sign of a good guard, my love. He's skulking in the shadows."

"Right," she said, laughing.

Upstairs she turned on the lights in the reception area, then walked down the hall with Declan right behind her. She flicked on the lights in her office, then frowned as she crossed the room to the fish tank.

"The filter is working fine," she said. "See? There's nothing wrong with it."

"Maybe it stopped, then started again. The guard just happened to see it when it shut down."

"I suppose that could happen, but I really don't know how these things work."

"Well, it's fine now, so we'd better get going. Bill will be expecting us."

"Don't worry," a deep voice said. "Bill has come to you."

Joy and Declan spun around, and Joy gasped when she saw Bill Cooper moving slowly into the room. There was a smile on his face.

And there was a gun in his hand.

"Dear God," she said, "what are you doing, Bill? Why do you have that gun pointed at us?"

"You aren't very adept at recognizing disguised voices on the telephone, Joy," Bill said.

"That was you? You posed as a security guard to get me here?"

"Not you, my dear. Declan. I followed you from here earlier and made sure he was still with you before I phoned. And now here he is, Declan Harris. As added insurance, I sent the invitations to the cocktail party to both of you. If I couldn't get you to come here, then I'd have you in my house. This is better, though. There will be no link between me and what takes place here."

"What are you talking about?" Declan asked, trying to calm his rapidly beating heart. "Why the gun, Bill?"

"The final curtain is at last, *at last,* going to come down. Oh, how long I've waited for this moment, how brilliantly I've played my role for two years. Of course, Mildred Fairchild is the real star of the show. She'll have top billing. Her name will be in the newspaper headlines in big, bold print."

"Wait a minute," Declan said. "What in the hell is going on here? If this is some kind of joke, it's not one bit funny."

"Joke!" Bill roared. "This has all been planned to the finest detail for one purpose. You, Declan Harris, are going to pay for the death of my son. You're going to die, just as Jeff did. If it weren't for you, he'd be alive today, here with me, where he belongs. You killed him, Declan. You killed my son!"

"I wasn't driving the damn car!" Declan yelled.

"Declan, don't," Joy said quietly. "Don't argue with him."

"You killed Jeff," Bill rushed on. "It was you who convinced him to take up architecture instead of becoming a doctor. From the day he was born I planned on Jeff being my partner. You ruined everything, Declan. You took him away from me, showed him a world that he knew nothing about, couldn't deal with. It's your fault he was in that fancy car, driving too fast, taking risks. A doctor would never jeopardize his own health and safety. No, never, because too many people are counting on him, trusting and believing in him. You twisted

Jeff's mind, altered his thinking, his values, everything. You killed him, Declan."

"My God," Declan muttered to Joy. "I can't believe this. He's out of his mind."

"Yes, he is," she whispered. "Be careful, Declan. Don't make him angry."

"Two years," Bill said, almost wistfully. "Such infinite patience I have. I had to wait for Mildred, dear Mildred, you see, to be released from the sanitarium. I played my role to perfection in the interim, appearing to be so grateful that you created that useless job for me, Declan. Then, as an added touch, I expressed fatherly concern over your stress level, making certain I mentioned it to your secretary, my nurse, and several others. No one will ever suspect me, as I've been like a doting father to Declan since Jeff was murdered by him. It's a shame that my dear friend Jack's daughter has to die, the lovely Joy, but that can't be helped. Mildred isn't well, you know. No, she isn't well at all. She still seeks revenge for the death of her daughter."

"What have you done to Mildred?" Declan asked.

"She has been, shall we say, a guest at my house, until I could put this final act into motion. She's fine. I haven't harmed her in any way."

"You broke into Declan's apartment," Joy said, "and poisoned Butch, as well as sending the letter and dog collar to Vince Santini."

"Me?" Bill laughed. "Oh, not me, Joy. Mildred did

all those things. See how clever I am? How intelligent I was to wait for her to be released? She'll be blamed for everything, including the death of one of the people she threatened two years ago. She will, of course, commit suicide. I want only Declan to die, but you know too much, Joy, so . . ." He sighed dramatically. "You will pay the price for what Declan did to my son. In actuality, it's Declan who is killing you, just as he killed Jeff."

"Bill," Joy said, her voice trembling slightly, "there's something you should know."

"What is it, dear?" Bill asked, raising his eyebrows.

"Remember how sorry you were that Jeff and I rarely saw each other after we grew up? Our busy schedules just didn't allow for it. But Jeff came to see me several years ago, Bill, and we had a long talk."

Bill frowned. "Why would a friendly chat be kept a secret? That's not nice."

"Jeff made me promise to keep our talk between just the two of us. You see, ever since he was a little boy he'd dreamed of becoming a doctor like you."

Declan stiffened. He'd seen a flicker of a shadow in the corridor. Was someone out in the hall? But who, and would they be able to help? Maybe he'd imagined the shadow. He had to protect Joy from Bill Cooper, had to do something. . . .

"Yes, a doctor," Bill said, nodding vigorously. "My

Jeff was going to be my partner. It was decided on the day he was born."

"Yes," Joy said, "Jeff wanted to be your partner. You were his idol, he worshiped you, said you were the finest doctor that had ever lived. His greatest fear was that he couldn't measure up to your standards, be as good as you expected him to be. He couldn't bear the thought of failing in your eyes. He knew, Bill, just how very much you expected of him."

"Jeff was brilliant," Bill said, his voice quivering. "He would have been a superb doctor."

"You told him that all of his life. He felt pressured, cornered, and became frightened that he wouldn't attain the level of expertise you expected of him. So, rather than let down the father he worshiped, he walked away from medicine before that could happen."

"What—what are you saying?"

"Oh, Bill, if only you hadn't set such high standards for Jeff. He felt defeated before he could even begin. If only you hadn't done that to your son."

Go for it, Joy, Declan thought. What a woman. There . . . yes, he'd seen it again, a shadow in the hall. There was definitely someone out in the corridor.

"Joy?" Bill said, nearly whining. "You're not saying this is my fault, are you? Are you, Joy? Declan did this. Declan took Jeff away from me."

"No, Bill," she said gently. "Jeff went to Declan because he had nowhere else to go. Jeff settled for being an architect, gave up his dream of making you proud of him, because you expected far, far too much of him. He went into Declan's world, was driving that car on that road, because you'd made him terrified of trying to enter *your* world and stand by your side. It troubled him deeply, and he finally came to me to sort through his inner anguish. His dream of becoming a doctor was forever beyond his reach."

A moan broke from Bill Cooper's lips, then a keening wail that seemed to tear at his soul. "No-o-o!"

At that instant the gun wavered in Bill's trembling hand. Suddenly Vince rushed into the office, launching himself at Bill. He hit the older man with a full body-block, crashing them both to the floor. The gun skidded across the carpet and under a chair. Bill Cooper went limp, then racking sobs consumed the older man as he covered his face with his hands.

Vince looked up at Joy and Declan. "It's all over," he said quietly. "He's a sad, sick man."

Declan drew Joy into his arms and held her tightly. "You were wonderful, unbelievable. You're the best psychologist in the city, the state . . . hell, the world. You also scared the living daylights out of me, lady, with your grandstand play, and I'm shaking all over. Oh, God, if anything had happened to you I . . . Don't ever do anything like that again."

"Okay," she said. "Declan, I can't breathe. You're squeezing the air out of me."

"Oh, I'm sorry."

"Are you two all right?" Vince asked, standing after he'd handcuffed Bill and picked up his gun.

"Yes," Joy said, "just badly frightened. Oh, what a nightmare this is. My heart aches for Bill when I think of the pain he's been in all this time. He's lived in a dark tunnel of confusion ever since Jeff died."

"Did Jeff really come to you?" Declan asked. "Tell you that he'd always wanted to be a doctor?"

"Yes, Declan, he did. Everything I just said to Bill was true. Jeff wasn't unhappy working with you, but it wasn't his true dream."

"I never knew. He didn't say one word, didn't give me any clue that he'd wanted to become a doctor like his father."

"Even though the two of you were best friends," she said, "he couldn't bring himself to discuss it with you. As time passed, he tried to lose himself in the fast-paced world he was living in."

Declan shook his head. "Unbelievable."

Vince crossed the room to Joy's desk. He dialed a number and a few moments later was giving instructions for an ambulance to come for Bill Cooper. After replacing the receiver, he turned to Joy and Declan again.

"You did a fantastic job here, Joy," he said. "You kept your cool and held things together. Want to be a cop?"

"No!" Declan said. "Shut up, Santini. No, don't

shut up. Explain how you happened to show up here."

"I got the search warrant to go into Mildred Fairchild's house. "She'd definitely been there."

"You knew that, didn't you?" Declan said. "Her sister called her about postponing her trip to Florida."

"Yes, but then Mildred disappeared. I knew she hadn't been near the place since I'd had it staked out. I went inside and what I found really bothered me. She had obviously left in a hurry."

"What do you mean?" Joy asked.

"There was half a cup of coffee on the table next to a plate of cookies. And there was an unfinished letter to her doctor saying how good it was to be home. She'd stopped writing in the middle of a sentence. But the biggy is that her purse was open on the chair. How many women leave the house without their purses?"

"Very few," Joy said. "They did a study on a college campus by having a fire drill in the middle of the night at several dormitories. Eighty-two percent of the male students grabbed their wallets before rushing outside. One hundred percent, every woman student, took her purse."

"You know fascinating things," Declan said, and kissed her on the temple.

"I take it that the kid here came out of the ether," Vince said to Joy, jerking his head in Declan's direction.

Joy smiled. "We both did."

"Good. Anyway, I kept the stakeout on Mildred's house, and late this afternoon she showed up. She'd managed to work the lock on the bedroom door where Bill had kept her since he'd forced her to go with him. Mildred had headed for her home to calm down and decide what to do. She was afraid no one would believe her story because of her past history. Believe me, I had no trouble buying her story, especially after I looked around inside Bill's house. I saw the stack of dishes from the meals he'd taken to Mildred and found the poison he'd used on Butch."

"But how did you know to come here?" Declan asked.

"I checked your place, then Joy's, then came here. I was going to go to your office next, Declan. If I couldn't find you anywhere, I was going to camp on your doorstep until you showed up. Bill had said enough to Mildred for me to know you were definitely in danger. Look, I'll finish up here. Declan, get your brilliant lady out of here. I'll get statements from you two later. You've been through enough for one night."

"We could stay until the ambulance comes, Vince," Joy said.

"No, go home."

Declan looked at Bill Cooper, who had quieted and was now curled into a fetal position on the floor. "This is still so hard to believe."

"He'll get the help he needs, Declan," Joy said. "My father will see to it, I'm sure. Bill will receive the finest care my father can find."

"Yes, he'll have a chance because of people like you. When I think of my stinking attitude toward your profession, I—"

"Hey," Vince said, punching Declan on the arm, "you're a little slow on the uptake, Harris, but when you figure things out, you're not so bad. Joy could do better but . . ." He shrugged. "What can I say? Go. I'll talk to you tomorrow."

Joy kissed Vince on the cheek. "Thank you, Vince. Good night."

"Don't kiss randy Italians," Declan said, grabbing her hand. "Their libido goes nuts. Italians are very hot-blooded, you know. Bye, Vince."

"See ya," Vince said quietly, then watched them leave. "Two by two, just like Noah's ark." He ran a hand over the back of his neck. "Forget it. I need some sleep, that's all."

The siren of an approaching ambulance cut through the silence in the room. Vince hunkered down next to Bill Cooper and placed one hand gently on the older man's shoulder.

The following night Declan held Joy's hand as he led her through a lush field, a multitude of stars twinkling above them. The fragrance of wildflowers wafted through the air.

"A picnic at night," Joy said, smiling. "This is so romantic, Declan, and such a lovely surprise."

"Well, I put in my eight hours at Harris and Cooper and declared that whatever was still on my drawing board could wait until tomorrow."

"Good for you. You're really getting a handle on stress management." She looked up at the sky. "The moon isn't full anymore. I guess that means it's no longer the blue moon."

"Do we need one?" Declan asked, spreading a blanket on the ground.

"Oh no, my love, we don't. I love you so much that even the Legend of the Blue Moon couldn't cause me to love you more. The blue moon worked its magic for us. I wonder who it will visit next?"

"I don't know. Oh, brother, would I laugh myself silly if Vince got caught in the magic of the blue moon. He's so darn smug about the fact that he'll never get involved in a serious relationship with a woman."

"The bigger they are, the . . ."

" 'Tis true. Here, come sit with me and see what great goodies I have packed in this picnic basket."

They ate their fill of fried chicken, potato salad, pickles, olives, crusty rolls, and chocolate chip cookies.

"I'm stuffed," Joy said, lying back on the blanket. "It all tasted so good."

Declan stretched out next to her and lay on his side, propping himself up on one forearm. He leaned over and gave her a quick, hard kiss.

"You taste better than chocolate chip cookies," he said.

She twined her arms around his neck. "What about chocolate chip ice cream?"

"You win, no contest. Why, Joy Marilee, you out-shine *mint* chocolate chip ice cream." He brushed his lips over hers. "You truly do."

"I swear, sir, you do say the most charming things." She tugged on his neck. "Kiss me, Declan."

"My pleasure, Joy."

And he kissed her. Their lighthearted moods were nudged aside by the burning desire within them that never seemed to be quelled. It continually glowed like smoldering embers ready to burst into hot flames at the slightest provocation: a look, touch, a mur-mured endearment.

"I want you," Declan said, close to Joy's lips. "There's no one here but us and the stars. Let me love you, Joy."

"Yes, oh yes, Declan. I want you too. I love you so very much."

"And I love you."

With an eagerness that engulfed them both, they shed their clothes and reached for each other. Lips and hands kissed and caressed as hearts thundered and passions soared.

"Declan, please," Joy murmured. "Come to me, Declan."

"Yes," he said. "Yes."

They became one beneath the silvery sky. In a rhythm perfectly matched, they moved together as one, sharing the intimate act that declared their love for all time. They teetered on the edge of ecstasy, then were flung far beyond reality to dance among the stars.

The wildflowers welcomed them as they drifted back.

"Oh, Declan," Joy whispered, "that was so beautiful."

He moved off her, then pulled her close, sifting his fingers through her silken hair.

"Yes, it was very beautiful." He paused. "Joy, I think I should tell you something."

"Oh?"

"This field is the one with the four-leaf clovers."

She burst into laughter. "*The* field? The one where cute little Declan Harris was created?"

"The very same."

"You planned this, didn't you?"

"Me?" he said, all innocence.

"Oh, you devil. I love you so much. I hope the four-leaf clovers work their magic for us just as they did for your parents."

"So do I and . . . listen, do you hear that? It's that

humming sound we heard when we first saw the blue moon. It started when we were talking about the magic of the four-leaf clovers."

"Yes, I hear it. It's so lovely. Strange, but lovely. It's . . . I don't know. It's as though it's magical music that comes only when something magical is happening. Am I making sense?"

"Wonderful sense," Declan said, then claimed her lips with his.

The humming continued for a few moments longer, then seemed to drift away as though going in search of the next recipient of magic. . . .

THE EDITOR'S CORNER

We've selected six LOVESWEPTs for next month that we feel sure will add to your joy and excitement as you rush into the holiday season.

The marvelously witty Billie Green leads off next month with a real sizzler, **BAD FOR EACH OTHER**, LOVESWEPT #372. Just picture yourself as lovely auburn-haired journalist Keely Durant. And imagine that your boss assigns you to interview an unbelievably attractive actor-musician, a man who makes millions of women swoon, Dylan Tate. Sounds fascinating, doesn't it? So why would the news of this assignment leave Keely on the verge of a collapse? Because five years before she and Dylan had been madly, wildly attracted to each other and had shared a white-hot love affair. Now, at their first reunion, the embers of passion glow and are quickly fanned to blazing flames, fed by sweet longing. But the haunting question remains: Is this glorious couple doomed to relive their past?

Please give a big and rousing welcome to brand-new author Joyce Anglin and her first LOVESWEPT #373, **FEELING THE FLAME**—a romance that delivers all its title promises! Joyce's hero, Mr. Tall, Dark, and Mysterious, was as charming to gorgeous Jordan Donner as he was thrilling to look at. He was also humorous. He was also supremely sexy. And, as it turned out, his name was Nicholas Estevis, and he was Jordan's new boss. Initially, she could manage to ignore his attractiveness, while vowing never to mix business with pleasure. But soon Nick shattered her defenses, claiming her body and soul. Passionate and apparently caring as he was, Jordan still suspected that love was a word only she used about their relationship. Would she ever hear him say the cherished word to her?

Sandra Chastain, that lovely lady from the land of moonlight and magnolias, seems to live and breathe
(continued)

romance. Next, in LOVESWEPT #374, **PENT-HOUSE SUITE,** Sandra is at her romantic Southern best creating two memorable lovers. At first they seem to be worlds apart in temperament. Kate Weston is a feisty gal who has vowed to fill her life with adventure upon adventure and never to stay put in one place for long. Max Sorrenson, a hunk with a bad-boy grin, has built a world for himself that is more safe than thrilling. When Kate and Max fall in love despite themselves, they make fireworks . . . while discovering that building a bridge to link their lives may be the greatest fun of all.

If ever there was a title that made me want to beg, borrow, or steal a book, it's Patt Bucheister's **ONCE BURNED, TWICE AS HOT,** LOVESWEPT #375. Rhys Jones, a good-looking, smooth operator, comes to exotic Hawaii in search of a mysterious woman. At first he doesn't guess that the strawberry blonde he bumped into is more than temptation in the flesh. She is part of what has brought him all the way from London. But more, the exquisite blonde is Lani . . . and she is as swept away by Rhys as he is by her. She soon learns that Rhys is everything she ever wanted, but will he threaten her happiness by forcing her to leave the world she loves?

Welcome back the handsome hunk who has been the subject of so many of your letters— *Kyle Surprise.* Here he comes in Deborah Smith's **SARA'S SURPRISE,** LOVESWEPT #376. Dr. Sara Scarborough saw that Kyle had gotten through the sophisticated security system that guarded her privacy. And she saw, of course, the terrible scars that he had brought back from their hellish imprisonment in Surador. Sara, too, had brought back wounds, the sort that stay buried inside the heart and mind. Demanding, determined, Kyle is soon close to Sara once more, close as they'd been in

(continued)

the prison. Yet now she has a "surprise" that could leave him breathless . . . just as breathless as the searing, elemental passion they share.

From first meeting—oops, make that impact—the lovers are charmed and charming in Judy Gill's thrilling **GOLDEN SWAN,** LOVESWEPT #377. Heroine B. J. Gray is one lady who is dynamite. Hero Cal Mixall is virile, dashing, and impossibly attracted to B.J. But suddenly, after reacting wildly to Cal's potent kisses, she realizes this is the man she's hated since she was a teenager and he'd laughed at her. Still, B.J. craves the sweet heat of him, even as she fears he'll remember the secret of her past. And Cal fears he has a job that is too tall an order: To convince B.J. to see herself as he sees her, as an alluring beauty. An unforgettable love story!

Do turn the page and enjoy our new feature that accompanies the Editor's Corner, our Fan of the Month. We think you'll enjoy getting acquainted with Patti Herwick.

As always at this season, we send you the same wishes. May your New Year be filled with all the best things in life—the company of good friends and family, peace and prosperity, and, of course, love. Warm wishes from all of us at LOVESWEPT.

Sincerely,

Carolyn Nichols

Carolyn Nichols
Editor
LOVESWEPT
Bantam Books
666 Fifth Avenue
New York, NY 10103

FAN OF THE MONTH

Patti Herwick

I first heard of LOVESWEPTs in a letter from Kay Hooper. We had been corresponding for some time when Kay told me she was going to start writing for Bantam LOVESWEPT. Naturally, since Kay was special—and still is—I was eager for the LOVESWEPTs to be published. I was hooked from then on. I read books for enjoyment. When a book comes complete with humor *and* a good story, I will buy it every time. As far as I'm concerned, LOVESWEPTs haven't ever changed. The outstanding authors that LOVESWEPT has under contract keep giving us readers better and more interesting stories. I am enchanted with the fantasy stories that Iris Johansen writes, the wonderful, happy stories that Joan Elliott Pickart writes, and, of course, Kay Hooper's. I can't say enough about Kay's work. She is a genius, her writing has gotten better and better. Every one of her books leaves me breathless. Sandra Brown is my favorite when it comes to sensual books, and I enjoy Fayrene Preston's books also. The fact that LOVESWEPTs are so innovative—with books like the Delaney series and Cherokee series—is another reason I enjoy reading LOVESWEPTs. I *like* different stories.

Now, as for me, I'm 44 years old, married, and have one grandchild. I think that I've been reading since the cradle! I like historical romances along with the LOVESWEPTs, and I probably read between 30 and 40 books a month. I became the proud owner of my own bookstore mostly because my husband said if I didn't do *something* about all my books, we were going to have to quit renting our upstairs apartment and let the books take over completely! I enjoy meeting other people who like to read, and I encourage my customers to talk about their likes and dislikes in the books. I never go *anywhere* without a book, and this has caused some problems. One time, while floating and reading happily on a swim mat in the water, I floated away. My husband got worried, searched, and when he found me and brought me back, he decided to do something so I wouldn't have the same problem again. Now he puts a soft nylon rope around the inflatable raft and *ties* it to the dock! I can only float 50 feet in any direction, but I can read to my heart's content.

I would like to thank LOVESWEPT for this wonderful honor. To have been asked to be a Fan of the Month is a memory I will treasure forever.

60 Minutes to a Better, More Beautiful You!

Now it's easier than ever to awaken your sensuality, stay slim forever—even make yourself irresistible. With Bantam's bestselling subliminal audio tapes, you're only 60 minutes away from a better, more beautiful you!

__	45004-2	**Slim Forever**	$8.95
__	45112-X	**Awaken Your Sensuality**	$7.95
__	45081-6	**You're Irresistible**	$7.95
__	45035-2	**Stop Smoking Forever**	$8.95
__	45130-8	**Develop Your Intuition**	$7.95
__	45022-0	**Positively Change Your Life**	$8.95
__	45154-5	**Get What You Want**	$7.95
__	45041-7	**Stress Free Forever**	$7.95
__	45106-5	**Get a Good Night's Sleep**	$7.95
__	45094-8	**Improve Your Concentration**	$7.95
__	45172-3	**Develop A Perfect Memory**	$8.95

NEW!

Handsome Book Covers Specially Designed To Fit Loveswept Books

Our new French Calf Vinyl book covers come in a set of three great colors— royal blue, scarlet red and kachina green.

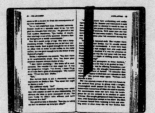

Each 7" × 9½" book cover has two deep vertical pockets, a handy sewn-in bookmark, and is soil and scratch resistant.

To order your set, use the form below.

THE DELANEY DYNASTY

Men and women whose loves an passions are so glorious
it takes many great romance novels by three bestselling
authors to tell their tempestuous stories.

THE SHAMROCK TRINITY

☐	21975	RAFE, THE MAVERICK *by Kay Hooper*	$2.95
☐	21976	YORK, THE RENEGADE *by Iris Johansen*	$2.95
☐	21977	BURKE, THE KINGPIN *by Fayrene Preston*	$2.95

THE DELANEYS OF KILLAROO

☐	21872	ADELAIDE, THE ENCHANTRESS *by Kay Hooper*	$2.75
☐	21873	MATILDA, THE ADVENTURESS *by Iris Johansen*	$2.75
☐	21874	SYDNEY, THE TEMPTRESS *by Fayrene Preston*	$2.75

THE DELANEYS: *The Untamed Years*

☐	21899	GOLDEN FLAMES *by Kay Hooper*	$3.50
☐	21898	WILD SILVER *by Iris Johansen*	$3.50
☐	21897	COPPER FIRE *by Fayrene Preston*	$3.50

Buy them at your local bookstore or use this page to order.

Bantam Books, Dept. SW7, 414 East Golf Road, Des Plaines, IL 60016

Please send me the items I have checked above. I am enclosing $_____
(please add $2.00 to cover postage and handling). Send check or money
order, no cash or C.O.D.s please.

Mr/Ms _____

Address _____

City/State _____ Zip _____

Please allow four to six weeks for delivery.
Prices and availability subject to change without notice.

Special Offer
Buy a Bantam Book
for only 50¢.

Now you can have Bantam's catalog filled with hundreds of titles plus take advantage of our unique and exciting bonus book offer. A special offer which gives you the opportunity to purchase a Bantam book for only 50¢. Here's how!

By ordering any five books at the regular price per order, you can also choose any other single book listed (up to a $5.95 value) for just 50¢. Some restrictions do apply, but for further details why not send for Bantam's catalog of titles today!

Just send us your name and address and we will send you a catalog!